SNOWFALL in Park City

❧ CHRISTMAS IN THE CANYONS ❦ BOOK TWO ❦

HOPE HOLLOWAY
AND
CECELIA SCOTT

Snowfall in Park City

Christmas in the Canyons Book 2

Hope Holloway and Cecelia Scott

Copyright © 2025 Hope Holloway

Christmas in the Canyons

Sleigh Bells in Park City
Snowfall in Park City
Mistletoe in Park City
Midnight in Park City

Chapter One

Nicole

For as long as Nicole Kessler could remember, snow had fallen on Christmas morning in the mountains surrounding Park City, Utah. This Christmas was no different, with flakes dancing beyond the picture windows of Snowberry Lodge, giving the pines their sugared edges and spreading a carpet of pure white over the canyons and peaks of the Wasatch Mountain Range.

Except this Christmas *was* different, Nicole thought with a secret smile. So different that she could physically feel the shift in her world, her heart squeezing every time she looked across the room and saw her parents snuggled close to each other on a plaid sofa.

Her father, Jack Kessler, championship skier, former ESPN color announcer, and prodigal ex-husband, had *not* slipped out on Christmas Eve, bound for his home in Vermont as they'd all expected.

Instead, after Nicole left last night to have a holiday celebration with her roommate and best friend, Brianna, Dad had changed his mind about going home. They all knew why—he and Mom were back together and still in love. After ten years of having divorced parents, Nicole's world felt complete again.

Holding that beautiful thought, she tucked her slipper-covered feet under her on the braided rug and wrapped both hands around a mug of marshmallow-topped cocoa. Her gaze roamed over the chaos of wrapping paper and ribbons that had been conquered by a ten-year-old and his brand-new puppy.

Christmas morning was glorious.

All around her, the people she loved most chatted and laughed while the logs popped and hissed in the stone fireplace and the massive tree glittered like a queen in her two-story castle.

Citrus and cranberry floated in from the kitchen, accompanied by the occasional burst of cold air when one of the lodge guests came in or out. They waved to the gathering and shared a chorus of, "Merry Christmas," as they passed, some stopping to fuss over the new dog or thank the family for the wonderful accommodations.

Over and over, Nicole caught her parents sharing a quiet look or brushing hands when they reached for their coffee. Or they would lean into each other like it was the most natural thing in the world, exchanging a soft whisper with the easy communication of a long-married couple.

Every time, Nicole felt as giddy as her little cousin half an hour ago when a furry, fluffy bundle of butterscotch curls came bounding in. Benny had nearly collapsed in ecstasy, proclaiming the puppy the "best Christmas present ever!"

Nicole had secretly hoped Jack and Cindy Kessler

might realize how much they missed each other when they were reunited. In fact, it was that hope that inspired Nicole to persuade her father to leave his home in Vermont and come back to Snowberry and run the sleigh rides...just for this Christmas season.

So, yeah, best Christmas present ever.

No doubt Nicole wore the same expression of pure delight that they'd all seen on little Benny's face when his Christmas dreams came true. The same look he wore now, with the little Cavalier-poodle mix curled on his lap, clearly having two speeds—zero and a hundred.

The puppy perked up at the scent of cinnamon when Nicole's Aunt MJ came in from the kitchen with a tray of rolls that smelled like they'd been made by the angels themselves.

A professional nurturer who ran Snowberry's kitchen and guest relations, Nicole's aunt had been up since dawn, bustling between the kitchen and the great room. Her job was to make sure the guests in the six cabins on the property and eight suites in the lodge were loved, fed, and happy. And she did it with style, grace, and the kindest, most cheerful heart ever created.

"Well, what are you going to call him, Benny?" MJ asked her beloved grandson as she perched on the armrest of a chair. "He sure looks like a teddy bear. How about Teddy or Smokey?"

Benny made a face, which was downright comical with his little glasses and childish features that simply didn't match his oddly mature personality. He stroked the curly, caramel-colored fur, thinking hard. "Honestly, Grandma, I want something that fits a real tech mogul's dog. Maybe Widget? Wi-Fi?"

They all laughed at that, well aware that he might be ten, but Benny had big plans and an IQ to match.

Red Starling, Nicole's grandfather, snorted from his armchair. "Back in my day, dogs were named Spot or Duke. None of this high-falutin' gizmo nonsense."

"Back in your day, Grumpy Santa wasn't an influencer." Nicole grinned at Red, who had a lifetime of experience and opinions and loved to share them all. "But now look at you. Viral sensation. Internet royalty."

A blush crept beneath Red's long, snowy beard—the same beard that had been the signature of @grumpysanta in Benny's TikToks. The two of them—great-grandfather and great-grandson and best pals—had created the account that not only broke Benny's "no phone" rule, but broke the internet, too. Well, enough to give Snowberry Lodge the attention it needed.

The videos had blown up, bookings had flooded in, and in the space of three weeks, the cabins and suites had filled. That meant the tax bill that had hung over their heads like a possible avalanche was officially covered and the check would go out next week.

Red harrumphed as if being an influencer at eighty-two was no big deal, but since the success, he walked a bit taller, cracked a few more jokes, and smiled without trying to hide it.

"Duke?" Benny repeated, his expression squishing as he shook his head. "He needs a name that sounds like a scientist, not a mayonnaise." The pup bark-chirped as if in agreement and tried to chew the ribbon from Benny's wrist.

"How about Rocket?" Jack suggested, lounging with his casual grace. He glanced sideways at Mom. "Fast, reliable, takes off like a shot."

"Or Cosmo," she countered, leaning into him. "Not the drink. The...universe."

"Byte," Nicole tossed in. "With a Y. Short and nerdy. Adorable."

"Make it Frostbyte," Gracie, Benny's mom, added to the fun. "It's a play on Christmas *and* your mother owns a bakery."

Behind his glasses, Benny's golden brown eyes lit up. "I kinda like that, Mom, but..." He looked down at his beloved pet. "He doesn't have white fur, so he doesn't look like a Frostbyte."

"'Cept we almost got a case of it when we got stuck out by the creek," Red said, reminding Benny of their recent misadventure on the sleigh.

Benny made a face. "Yeah. I don't think I want to remember that. I need a better name."

"How about Pixel?" The question came from out in the hall, where a man stood holding a platter.

"Thank you, Matt," MJ said, rushing to take it from him. "I appreciate the help."

Matt Walker, the older guest staying in Cabin Five since Thanksgiving, had been in and out of the kitchen with MJ all morning.

As always, he wore a quietly expensive sweater

Nicole suspected didn't come from the Main Street tourist shops. He and MJ had been laughing a lot lately and, today, he'd lingered all morning.

Well, he *was* alone on Christmas, which was sad and...curious. Why was he here at a ski lodge in the mountains by himself for a month now? And showing no signs of leaving?

Before she could give it much thought, the naming suggestions heated up, stealing her attention.

"Chip?" Jack tried when Benny rejected Matt's suggestion of Pixel because it sounded too much like a movie studio.

"Cache or Cookie?" Cindy suggested, the two of them obviously having a grand time making up names.

"How about a famous scientist or computer nerd?" MJ asked. "Like Einstein."

"Or Woz," Nicole offered. "As in Steve Wozniak."

"Whoever that is," Red grumbled.

"Einstein's good," Benny admitted. "But a little obvious." He buried his face in the puppy's fur, the dog licking his chin. "What's your name, little fellow?"

"You think some more and we'll do another round of presents," MJ suggested, already half turned toward the kitchen. "I've got a quiche that needs to come out of the oven that I promised to the folks in Cabin Three. I know they usually come to us and eat in the dining room, but everyone wants to respect our family time, so I'm taking some things out to them."

"You're the best." Cindy blew a kiss to her sister. "And if you need help—"

"I'm helping her," Matt said. "Y'all just relax and enjoy your Christmas."

MJ turned and gave him the warmest smile, her crystal blue eyes looking especially bright this morning and her auburn hair styled as neat as Nicole could remember seeing it. She even had a little makeup on.

Was that Christmas morning...or Matt Walker?

"This one's from you, Nicole!" Benny shouted, sliding an oversized envelope from under the tree. "It has paw prints on it and says 'for my cousin.'" He looked over the rims of his glasses. "Actually, you and my mom are cousins. We are first cousins once—"

"Removed," she finished for him, giving him a playful nudge. "I *know*, Benny. Open your present. It might be for you and...Debug."

"Debug." He giggled and pointed the envelope at her. "I don't hate that." Then, he tore at the paper, frowning at the words on the certificate he pulled out. "One Week At Paws & Pals Winter Training Camp!" he exclaimed, looking almost as excited as he had been for the dog. "It's this week! Dog training school at Canine Canyon Refuge!" He turned to his mother. "Can I go?"

"Of course," Gracie exclaimed. "That's the refuge where we got...Em-dash."

He scanned the page. "This is so cool, Nicole! I can teach him to sit and roll over and give me a paw."

"And go outside to do all his business," Nicole added, winking at Gracie. "So, it's really for both of you."

"Thank you," her cousin mouthed.

"They offer the class to kids who got dogs for Christmas," Benny said as he read the flyer. "Listen! 'Four- and two-legged students attend obedience basics followed by winter play and leash walks. Listen to a vet teach the How to Be a Good Dog Owner workshop. Best of all, Puppy Pals Social Hour with hot chocolate for humans and tiny biscuits for the dogs.'"

"Now that's a great way to spend winter vacation," Red said. "I think I'd like to go."

"You can come with me, Grandpa!" Benny cooed, always ready to make room for his beloved great-grandfather.

"Oh, I think it's for kids only," Gracie said quickly. "But you can teach us all what you and, um, Crash learn."

He looked up, the joy tempered by trepidation. "Lots of kids?" he asked, trying to sound casual but Nicole knew he wasn't.

"Whoever got a dog for Christmas," Nicole said, stealing a glance at Gracie.

They'd discussed Benny's struggles with making friends, and this gift was meant to help that issue. Gracie knew it, but Benny had no idea there was an ulterior motive.

He accepted the answer and clutched the envelope to his chest, squishing the puppy, who didn't mind. "We're going to training school together, buddy! Just you and me!"

As one of the last gifts came out from under the tree, Nicole's phone buzzed in her pocket and she winced at the interruption. She'd left her number on the door of the ski shed, the rental and sales business she ran here at Snowberry, in case anyone needed her.

Most of the lodge guests who wanted to ski today had picked up their equipment yesterday, so she didn't expect to have to go to work on Christmas Day.

But someone from an unknown number asked if the Snowberry Lodge Adventure Shack was open for rentals, so she pushed up from her comfy seat.

"Be right back, fam," she announced. "Duty calls. But do not pick a name without me, Benny!"

She slipped into the kitchen and hopped into her boots by the mudroom door. Grabbing her parka, she pulled on a stocking cap with a cheerful white tassel and stepped into the quiet bite of cold outside.

With this morning's fresh powder over last night's packed crust, the air felt unnaturally crisp and thin, like a perfect mountain morning.

The Snowberry Sleigh sat just off the drive, a thin mantle of white on its curved runners and red side panels. Her horse, Copper, was tucked inside the stable, having been brushed, fed, and blanketed when Nicole arrived from her townhouse early this morning.

She patted the sleigh's rail as she passed, the paint smooth and cold, loving the old antique beast that had brought her father home—and kept him here.

Still smiling, she crossed the wide, plowed path and headed toward the ski shed, her kingdom and workplace. The old barn's giant door was closed, with a man standing next to it, blowing into bare hands. As he turned, she caught sight of the red cross on the side of his jacket.

She came to a sudden stop and sucked in an icy breath when she realized that it was Cameron. Or, as she and her friend, Brianna, called him—"the hot ski patrol guy."

What was he doing here, standing outside the shed, head tipped back to watch the lazy spirals of snow?

Not only was she surprised by that—but the reaction that danced through her whole body was a little shocking, too. She couldn't fight her smile at the sight of him.

"Skiing emergency bring you all the way out here?" she called, taking careful steps so she didn't face plant in front of him. Not that it would be the first time—he'd seen her take a few nasty falls as she learned to renegotiate the easiest runs at Deer Valley over the last few weeks.

He laughed, and even from a distance, his smile made her toes curl in her boots.

"My skis caught fire," he joked. "No, wait, that was me on Daly's this morning." He touched his finger to his tongue, then his shoulder, and hissed. "Smokin'."

She had to laugh, despite the interruption to her delightful morning. Mostly because it just got even more delightful.

"Of course you'd sail down Deer Valley's toughest run," she said. "You're such a ski dude."

"Why do I think that's not a compliment?"

She came a little closer, feeling the impact of his deep

blue eyes pinned on her. She'd only seen him twice in her life, but his eyes were unforgettable, and so was the just-a-little-too-long dirty blond hair that brushed the collar of his red ski parka.

"It's just an observation," she said. "What are you doing here on Christmas morning?"

"Merry Christmas to you, too, Nicole Kessler."

He knew her last name? Oh, yes—he'd met her the first time with Dad, who he'd recognized. Was he here on Christmas morning...as a Jack Kessler fan?

Because that would be a bit of a disappointment.

"I saw your friend Brianna at Deer Valley this morning," he explained. "She gave me a present." He held out his phone. "Your number and place of business. I wasn't sure if she was being real, so I decided to test the truth of both. Looks like your friend is honest."

Somehow, she managed to play it cool, knowing Brianna was definitely skiing this Christmas morning. Her folks had gone to Sweden for the holidays and that girl chose the slopes over anything—even Christmas here at Snowberry Lodge.

"Yeah, well, Bri's honest to a fault," she said, "and frequently sticks her nose where it doesn't belong."

"I begged," he said, the two words so sweet and humble and honest that her heart went shamelessly light.

"She also said you'd be with your family," he added quickly. "So if I'm intruding, say the word and I'm a streak in the snow. I just—" He rubbed the back of his neck, the picture of a man who'd rather ski a double-black blindfolded than overshare feelings. "After this morning's early shift, which I just finished, I have the rest of the week off. And I thought maybe if you had a sliver of time between your yuletide celebrations, we could...hang out?"

She laughed a little, thinking "yuletide" was more a word Benny or even Red would use, not this too-cool-for-school ski patrol boy. Well, not a boy. He looked to be in his late twenties or so, maybe a couple years older than Nicole.

"Bri said you're off the rest of this week, too," he added with a meaningful raise of a brow. "So..."

"She's a menace," Nicole muttered, laughing.

"Well?"

As if she'd say no. "I could be convinced," she said, drawing the words out to at least pretend she wasn't half panting at the idea.

"Tomorrow afternoon?" he suggested. "We could walk Main Street. Get hot chocolate. Secretly mock the tourists?"

"Who make both of our jobs possible," she reminded him.

He tipped his head, suitably chastised. "No mocking, then. Just hot chocolate and a fine Park City vibe."

She smiled and nodded. "Tomorrow works. I'll meet you at Sugarfall."

"The bakery?"

"My cousin Gracie owns it."

"Whoa, perks. Yes, I'll see you there at...one o'clock?"

"Perfect." She let out a quick breath and gestured to the lodge behind her. "Do you want to meet my—"

He held up a hand and shook his head. "Not a chance I'm going to interrupt your Christmas. And some...one is waiting for me. See you tomorrow," he said, a soft light in his eyes. "Merry Christmas, Nicole."

"Merry Christmas," she echoed.

He took a step backward, then another, as if he were reluctant to turn his back on her. Finally, he pivoted and jogged down the path, leaving boot prints in the layer of new snow.

Nicole closed her eyes and fought the urge to dance. Cameron was cute and sweet and, *whoa*, this Christmas kept getting better.

A minute later, she stepped back through the kitchen door. After taking off her boots and jacket but leaving her stocking hat on because it was silly and festive, she headed back to the living room. There, Benny stood in front of the coffee table like he was giving a TED talk.

"I have made my decision," he announced, chin up, puppy perched on his forearm like a furry loaf with ears. "His official, legal, and forever name is Sir Isaac Newton."

A beat of stunned silence, and then the room detonated into laughter and applause.

"Isaac Newton?" Red asked with a chuckle.

"*Sir*," Benny confirmed, deadly serious. "The 'Sir' is important."

Jack clapped his hands together once, delighted. "We can call him Newt for short. Or...Zach?"

Benny hugged the dog closer and shook his head vehemently. "No nicknames. He has a title. From the

Queen. Or King. I don't know but I'll look it up on Grandpa's new phone."

"The one you're not supposed to touch," Red murmured into his coffee cup. "Because you lost the *last* one you weren't supposed to touch in the snow."

"Sir Isaac Newton it is," Nicole agreed, because how could it be anything else?

She bent to kiss the top of Benny's head. The puppy licked the air near her nose, woofed once, and swatted a playful paw at her stocking cap tassel.

"He's going to graduate first in his class," Benny said, his face the picture of seriousness. "Right, Sir Isaac Newton?"

"You're gonna want to shorten that, Benny," Gracie said. "That name is a mouthful."

"Nope," Benny said. "He's a knight of the Cavapoo order."

Laughter rolled around the room again, as warm and cozy as the fire and the mess of wrapping paper that no one bothered to worry about. Across the room, her father inched closer to her mother to say something in her ear, and Mom turned her face toward him.

Their noses were inches apart. Their hands were nearly touching. It was the kind of almost-kiss moment that could last forever or end in a heartbeat. And then— like the scene had been scripted by a benevolent universe —they both leaned that last inch and took that kiss.

Not deep or dramatic or embarrassing, just the soft, sure press of two people who'd circled back to the same page after a long time in the wrong chapter.

Joy rose in Nicole's chest. She looked out the window and watched a single flake flutter and fall, landing on a pine branch.

It always snowed on Christmas morning, but this one, and the week ahead, felt so different from the rest. She couldn't wait to find out why.

Chapter Two
MJ

By the time the Christmas sky had gone dark and the outside tree lights blinked on one by one, MJ McBride settled into her quiet kitchen to relish the simple joy of preparing for tomorrow's breakfast. With no vacancies in Snowberry Lodge, her tasks were many, but she certainly wouldn't complain.

Instead, she whispered the words to her favorite Christmas song—not that she'd admit that to anyone but George McBride. She smiled at the thought of her late husband, gone from her life for five years, but never far from her heart.

He loved to tease her and call her "Mariah" when she'd happily hum "All I Want for Christmas is You." Remembering how he'd laugh and point to himself and say, "Me?" when she sang it, she rolled her shoulders and hummed to nobody but her still-vivid memories.

Long ago, when she was a much younger woman, they'd dance right here when no one was around, and if George had his one glass of Christmas bourbon, he'd croon the high notes into a wooden spoon. She'd roll her eyes and give him a hug, loving him more than life itself.

"Oh, George," she sighed. "I'm not going to get what

I want for Christmas, which would be one more dance. But I wouldn't mind if you'd help us get through the next year without my sister threatening to sell this place."

Yes, that was a good Christmas wish. Cindy had mellowed slightly, since their December was such a success and the tax bill was covered. But MJ knew her younger sister was already thinking about next year and the renovations they needed to do. She was the brains of Snowberry, but MJ was the heart.

And if they ended up selling because they got too deep in the hole, that heart would break.

She whisked eggs and milk and cream with vanilla—the base for tomorrow's Boxing Day French toast—and poured the sunshine-yellow mixture in two buttered pans.

She tucked a foil cover over the pans and slid them onto the rack in the giant fridge, her mind ticking through all the things this lodge full of guests might need tomorrow. A few people had gathered in the living room earlier and had cocktails and snacks, but being Christmas, the schedule was a little different.

She'd liked that change from the routine.

Also—if she were honest with herself—*something* had her a touch giddier than usual, and it wasn't just the holidays, although they helped.

Something made the song lodge in her throat when she sang it, she had to admit. It wasn't only that Red's Grumpy Santa had "made December" and paid the tax bill, or that she'd caught a glimpse of her sister looking at

Jack the way she had when they first met thirty-some years ago.

It was...*well*. She had a very hard time even thinking about it, or saying it in her head.

She wiped her hands on a towel and told herself she shouldn't think about—

The back door creaked, and a swirl of cold air came in with a man who had taken to slipping through this space like he was family.

She shouldn't think about *him*.

"Knock-knock." Matt Walker's chestnut hair was dusted with snowflakes and streaked with silver threads which she, a woman of sixty-two with some silver threads of her own, found very attractive.

Around a golden mustache, his cheeks were ruddy, the color deepened by his Florida tan that hadn't yet disappeared during his weeks in Utah.

As he slipped out of a down jacket and hung it on a hook, MJ couldn't help noticing that for all his expensive clothes and good manners, he moved like a man who'd used his body for something other than sitting.

Like someone once rough around the edges who'd worked to smooth them out.

Matt had never said exactly what he did for a living other than he'd "owned a business," but he didn't act like a lofty executive. He was easy on his feet, and capable, with hands that showed an honest trade in their knuckles and palms.

Not that she'd spent *that* much time studying his hands.

"Hey, there," MJ said, her voice a little too cheerful even for her. "You're either hungry or lost."

"Not after a long day of grazing," he answered. "Although..." He took a sniff. "Does this kitchen ever *not* smell like cinnamon and calories?"

She chuckled. "It's Christmas, so there's plenty of both."

She leaned back and crossed her arms, smiling at the man who'd been at Snowberry Lodge for a month now, and spent plenty of time in here casually visiting her. She never minded, though.

"Actually," he said, "I came to deliver a Christmas present for the lodge."

Her brows lifted. "Really? You didn't have to do that."

"Well, I've become a fixture here and I know you've turned down some would-be guests who would like my very nice mountain-view cabin."

"You're not staying here for *free*," she reminded him on a laugh, knowing he was paying top Park City dollar for that cabin.

He lifted a shoulder, the smallest flicker of mischief crossing his face. "But I have a gift. For you. And Cindy. And...the lodge."

"Okay." She wiped her hands on her apron. "Cindy and Jack are in the living room—"

"No, I'm right here," Cindy called, coming down the hall. "We need more cocoa and Jack's stoking the fire—" She slowed and smiled at their guest. "Hello, Matt."

"He has a present for us," MJ blurted, oddly excited

at the idea, even though it was probably a vase or a picture or some token for the lodge.

"For us?" Cindy brushed some of her pale blond hair over her shoulder, a glint in her blue eyes that MJ hadn't seen since...well, since before the divorce that never should have happened. "That was so kind of you, Matt."

"Then let's step outside," he said. "Grab a coat."

MJ and Cindy shared a look of anticipation and surprise, grabbing their jackets and sliding into their respective boots lined up under the mudroom bench.

He waited at the door like a gentleman, his soft brown eyes downright merry.

MJ liked a man who enjoyed giving a gift. It said something about his generous heart and a kind desire to see others happy. George had been like that, she mused as they stepped outside.

The night air stung MJ's face, cold and clean, spiced with pine from the dozens of well-lit evergreens that filled the property.

"It's in the front," he said, leading them that way, past the sleigh and the ski shed, to the main entrance of the lodge.

The porch lights threw soft halos on the snow-covered drive. Down the hill, a set of taillights winked as a large delivery truck returned to the main road.

"I didn't hear a truck," MJ said under her breath, a frown forming as she followed Matt.

"What..." Cindy gasped, eyes narrowing as they tracked to the long, low shape just beyond the end of the front steps. A tarp lay in a neat spill beside it, abandoned like a coat dropped in an eager moment. "Is that..."

MJ didn't need a second look. She recognized the silhouette. A laugh started somewhere in her chest. "*No.*"

"Yes," Matt said, grinning with excitement and relief, as if keeping a secret all day had been painful.

"No!" MJ repeated, not quite able to process that she was looking at a brand-new, state-of-the-art, utterly spectacular *snowmobile.*

Oh, no, this was not the battered old beast they'd tried to coax through last winter—it died a tragic death in March.

This was not the second-, third-, or fourth-hand salvage Red swore he could fix with a wrench and a prayer.

This was glossy and muscular, with a wide track meant to float over whatever Mother Nature threw at them, two seats with backing, a cargo rack, all shiny and perfect and new.

This was a snowmobile that no one at Snowberry Lodge could afford...but, obviously, Matt Walker could.

She put a hand to her mouth. "Matt," she said, and then said it again because the first time didn't do the job. "*Matt.*"

He smiled down at her with an expression she couldn't quite read. It was the look of a man who'd done a good thing and wanted to fist pump but was too humble to do so.

"You said last week you used to have one," he reminded her. "And when Benny and Red got into that jam in the meadow, you told me the UTV had a rough time on the snow and ice, as would be expected. So…"

"So you bought us a brand-new snowmobile?" MJ asked, her voice rising in disbelief she couldn't hide.

"Well, I thought a place like this needs the right machine. For safety. For guests. For peace of mind." He slid his hands into his coat pockets. "Just seemed like the right thing to do."

The right thing? It was…well, she didn't have a word for that level of generosity.

Her sister walked closer to the vehicle, stared at it, let her jaw loosen, but she seemed…stiff. Maybe uncomfortable, but who wouldn't be at the magnitude of this gift?

"This is amazing and…*amazing*." Cindy huffed an awkward laugh, but her smile faded. "I just don't think we can accept this, Matt."

"We can't?" MJ asked, her fingers splayed over her heart, feeling the beat even under her down jacket.

"Because it's…too much."

"Well, I thought you might say that, and I didn't mean to go overboard, but I want to give it to you." He shifted his weight in his boots, looking like he might have actually practiced this speech. "Sometimes a gift is as much about the giving as the receiving. And it's Christmas. So, Merry Christmas. Please accept it and use it in good health."

"Oh, Matt." MJ sighed, feeling a little lightheaded. "That is so gracious and kind. Thoughtful doesn't begin to cover it. Thank you."

Under his mustache, his lips pulled into a smile.

"Hopefully, you won't have to save another old man and young boy, but if you do"—he jutted his chin toward the snowmobile—"this should come in handy."

Now, *that* was an understatement.

He glanced at Cindy, whose expression was softening, but still uncertain. "There's a manual in the storage bin," he said. "And the dealer said he's happy to come out for a tutorial at your convenience."

Cindy exhaled, her breath coming out in a puff. "I honestly don't know what to say," she admitted. "It's extraordinary."

"You need it, right?"

"Need it?" she scoffed. "Yes. It's almost a liability *not* to have one out here."

"Then here you go." He reached into his pocket and pulled out a set of keys, holding them out to MJ. "I'd say take her for a spin, but you probably want to wait until daytime. Although it has great LED lights."

Somewhere under her happy shock, a little spark caught and flared—the way he saw what they needed, not because they'd asked but because he'd been paying attention. MJ's heart tightened in her chest, a mix of gratitude and affection and, God help her, attraction.

There it was. The thing she didn't want to admit.

"Won't you come in and let us ply you with treats and maybe some mulled wine?" she suggested. "Please. Some tea and gingerbread cookies. Anything."

He lifted both palms, apologetic but not evasive. "I'd love to, but not tonight. I'm going into town. But thank you."

Cindy's chin tipped a fraction. "Matt, please let us pay you something or..." Her voice faded as though she knew, like MJ, the plea would fall on deaf ears. "We'll comp your cabin."

"You will not!" he exclaimed. "I know about the tax money and all." At Cindy's look, he chuckled. "I got a tendency to blend into the background and I've been picking this sweet lady's brain while she tried to cook..." He smiled at MJ. "I'm aware that you're swimming against the tide. Now you can fly right over it on this fine vehicle."

"But..."

He shook his head. "Honestly, I really just like it here and this..." He shifted his gaze to the snowmobile, a definite glow in his light brown eyes. "This makes me happy."

He sighed out those words as if...as if he'd been searching for something to make him happy and somehow that had led him to a snowmobile.

"Well, I call it a Christmas miracle," MJ said on a laugh, trying to lighten the moment.

He smiled, walking toward the snowmobile. "No miracles, just...good luck."

"We're so grateful," MJ said, hating that she sounded like a breathless teenager and not a woman in her sixth decade of life.

"We really are," Cindy add. "Grateful and overwhelmed."

He tapped the headlight casing and smiled down at the beast. He glanced at her again, holding her gaze for a few heartbeats, then nodded. "Happy to hear that. Merry Christmas to the ladies of Snowberry Lodge."

"Merry Christmas," MJ whispered. Cindy echoed it, polite and warm, but MJ heard a thin note of worry in her sister's voice. Maybe not worry...maybe doubt.

They watched him stride toward the high-end SUV he'd parked near the ski shed lot. He popped a hand in the air without turning and slid behind the wheel, and in a minute the taillights disappeared into the dark toward town.

For a long time, MJ and Cindy stood in silence, as though neither one of them knew what to say. As much as MJ wanted to jump up and down on the snow, she just waited for Cindy's response.

It finally came as a soft laugh. "*What* just happened, MJ?"

MJ laughed, disbelief bubbling out. "He bought us a snowmobile," she said, stating the obvious and the impossible. "A beautiful, practical, perfect snowmobile."

Cindy grunted softly. "I've priced these, MJ. This is... whoa. I can't even wrap my head around it."

"We needed it, Cin."

"But what's the catch? It can't be free." She tipped her head. "Two words, sister of mine. Henry Lassiter."

MJ winced at the mention of the stranger who'd nearly scammed them a few days ago. But MJ had recognized the man and stopped them from making the most expensive mistake in Snowberry's history.

"I understand you're scarred from that experience,

Cindy. But Matt is nothing like Henry. He's not asking for anything."

"I guess," Cindy conceded, because she was fair and practical and didn't argue with facts. "But it also raises questions."

They stood there another minute, but it got cold and the front door opened and Jack stepped outside.

"What is this?" he asked, jogging coatless down the steps. "Where did you get this?"

The two women shared a look.

"Santa Claus," MJ joked.

"Who isn't real," Cindy countered.

Even MJ had to admit something was a little off about this gift—or maybe it was the man who gave it. She didn't know, and couldn't understand why she felt like she had to defend this guy she barely knew. And secretly liked.

AFTER JACK CHECKED out the machine and made suitably male comments about things like horsepower and torque, they gathered at the kitchen table.

While MJ made cocoa, she and Cindy told him everything.

"Well, that's, uh, quite a gift," he said. "He must like you, MJ."

"Stop it." She set his cocoa in front of him with an exaggerated scowl.

He grinned at her in that brotherly way she used to

always love during the years they shared as in-laws. MJ and Jack had a connection all their own, and it felt good to have his warmth and wry humor back in their lives.

After MJ sat across the table from them with her own mug of hot chocolate, Cindy sighed noisily.

"What?" MJ said, squirming under the pragmatic and sensible gaze of her level-headed sister.

Cindy's brows flicked. "Why don't you share everything you know about Mr. Matt Walker?"

"Oh, here we go," MJ groaned. "The inquisition."

"Mary Jane Starling McBride," Cindy said, not laughing. "You know as well as I do that two sixty-year-old women who co-own twenty-five acres of prime real estate on the outskirts of Park City are like a couple of sitting ducks. We have to be careful."

MJ sighed, shaking her head but unable to disagree with that. "I just don't have that feeling about him," she said. "I sniffed out that Lassiter character the minute you mentioned his deal."

Cindy made a face. "Which just proves it's easy for *both* of us to get snookered."

"No one is getting snookered," Jack said, putting a calming hand on Cindy's back. "But I would like to know more about the guy, MJ. What has he shared?"

"Not much," she admitted, hating that the words made Cindy lift a dubious brow. "He's from Florida."

"Where in Florida?" Jack asked.

She shrugged, chuckling. "Just...Florida. I don't know Miami from Orlando, Tampa, or...name another city there. Honestly, it's like another country to me, one I've never visited. Obviously, it's sunny and warm because he's tan."

"And staying in an obscure mountain resort for the entire holiday season," Cindy said. "All by himself."

"That doesn't make him a serial killer, Cin," MJ shot back. "Or a con artist."

"I know, I know," Cindy assured her, her voice softening with Jack's touch. "What else has he told you?"

She thought about it. "He's retired."

"From?"

MJ grimaced. She had no earthly idea. "He owned a business. Don't ask what because he didn't tell me. But I didn't ask. It would have seemed like I was..."

"Like you were what?" Cindy pressed.

"I don't want him to think I'm, you know... interested."

"Asking him about his business isn't flirting," Jack told her.

"But I understand," Cindy said sweetly, putting a hand on MJ's. "You're very friendly with every person who stays here, and a single man might take that the wrong way from an attractive woman like you."

She snorted. "Attractive? Now you're stretching it."

"MJ!" Cindy leaned in. "With all that gorgeous hair you try to keep in a bun and glowing skin from natural joy and the prettiest blue eyes for miles? You're in shape, you're happy as a clam, and your cooking could bring a man to his knees."

"I agree," Jack chimed in. "You're a catch."

"A catch?" She looked from one to the other and

almost laughed out loud. "If you're fishing for a sixty-two-year-old widow, maybe."

"We don't know what he's fishing for," Cindy said.

"Well, he simply hasn't shared a lot about himself, but I guess I can ask. I mean, now that he's bought us a snowmobile."

"We could do a little digging," Jack said slowly. "People's lives are all over the internet."

MJ drew back. "No! That really feels intrusive. He's a paying guest."

"In *cash*," Cindy said, dragging the word out like it was a federal indictment.

"People pay in cash," MJ said. "We've had plenty of cash guests."

"But not one who gave us a brand-new snowmobile."

So true. "I definitely get the sense that he has some... wealth," MJ said, thinking about the small clues she'd picked up. "Not that he's flashy or anything, but he did have dry cleaning delivered, and when I grabbed the hangers from the door, I noticed very expensive labels. Italian." She swallowed. "That doesn't make him a... swindler."

Cindy nodded, thinking as she ran her finger along the rim of her cup.

"He spends a lot of time with you," Cindy said.

"He's comfortable in a kitchen, I think," MJ replied. "He asks about recipes, about the lodge, about our history. He is always offering to help, too. He doesn't act rich."

"He *gifts* rich," Cindy murmured.

"He acts like a working man," MJ continued. "Like, have you ever noticed his hands?"

"No, but apparently you have," Cindy teased.

"They're working hands. Not office hands. He's done something in his life that involved building or fixing or hauling."

"So he could haul our lodge right out from under us," Cindy said, only half kidding.

"Cindy." MJ plopped her elbows on the table. "You can't think that every man who shows an interest in this place is Henry Lassiter, out to take our money and legacy."

"You're right," she agreed. "I'm traumatized because I almost handed a complete stranger fifty thousand dollars."

"But you *didn't*," MJ said. "I don't think we have anything to worry about with Matt, and I really don't want to run off and hire a PI because the man uses cash and is generous."

Jack snorted. "I was thinking Google, not...Hercule Poirot."

Cindy and MJ smiled at that.

"He hasn't asked for anything," MJ said.

"People who want something don't always announce it," Cindy said. "Sometimes they start by finding the heart and coming in that way. He already knows we're in financial trouble."

"We haven't tried to hide it." MJ picked up her mug, wondering how much she had told him in those easy conversations at the kitchen island.

"Will you at least talk to him?" Cindy asked. "Maybe learn a little more? Find out where he lives in Florida. What he used to do. Whether Matt Walker is his real name."

"Cindy."

"He could be a novelist traveling under a pen name," Cindy said, raising both hands to make her point. "He could be the world's nicest con man. He could be in witness protection. I don't know. I just...don't want to be naïve again."

MJ nodded. "I will, I promise. But it has to happen naturally. I'm not going to grill him or Google him. And neither will you."

"I won't." Cindy nodded and reached out, her touch on MJ's arm as binding as a handshake. "I promise."

MJ nodded. They were as close as sisters could be, and when they made a promise, they kept it.

Then Cindy stood and came around to kiss her cheek. "And I'm sorry to be the Grinch."

"You're not the Grinch," MJ said into her sister's hair that grazed her cheek. "I promise I'll find out more about him."

"Good," Cindy said, looking at Jack. "Weren't we going to take a moonlight walk in the snow about an hour ago?"

"Walk?" he scoffed. "Woman, there's a shiny new snowmobile out there waiting for us. It's a total upgrade from the sleigh or the UTV."

Her face brightened. "Can we?" Cindy asked MJ.

She laughed. "Unless you think he put a tracker on it and will follow you and kill you in the woods."

Cindy gasped.

"The keys are on the counter," MJ said. "Go fly through Snowberry and make out like a couple of teenagers."

They looked at each other like that was exactly what they had planned, laughing as they put on their coats and boots and found the keys.

"Love you, Mary Jane!" Cindy called out as they left.

MJ smiled at the name only Cindy used in their closest of moments. Then, she sat very still at the table, listening for the rumble of the snowmobile as it started. She heard it in a few minutes, a low growl of muscle and power.

After a minute, it faded in the distance and left her in the utter quiet of her kitchen on Christmas night.

Getting up, MJ finished her breakfast preparation, cleaned the cups in the sink, and wiped down the counters until they gleamed, humming her favorite Christmas song.

"All I want for Christmas," she whispered, stopping at the window to look out at the snow, "is...the truth."

She sighed. Cindy was right. There was a place for optimism and the benefit of the doubt, but that gift was over the top and she hoped she could find out why.

And really hoped that she liked the answer.

Chapter Three

Gracie

The morning after Christmas, the snow had finally stopped, leaving Park City skiers happy and tourists able to enjoy a blindingly sunny day in town. Snow stacked on fence rails and pine boughs, the sky glistened like a blue dome, and all the roads along the outskirts had been plowed into neat corridors as Gracie drove to Canine Canyon Refuge.

She eased her van into the turn lane, the heater purring high enough to fog the edges of the windshield. In the rearview mirror she caught Benny's profile—serious as a scientist—his knit hat pulled low over shaggy brown hair, his gloved hand absently stroking the silky ears of Sir Isaac Newton.

The puppy wore a tiny harness clipped to the seatbelt so he couldn't lunge face-first into the front seat, which they'd learned the hard way he liked to do.

He was six months of Cavapoo exuberance, equal parts curl and curiosity, and a whole lot of love. Gracie didn't think Benny had let go of the dog in twenty-four hours except to bathe, eat, and sleep.

"You excited?" she asked. "Paws & Pals, Day One."

"Excited about the curriculum," he said without

looking up, the use of a word like "curriculum" not even fazing Gracie. She knew when Benny was about six months old that he was smart. The word "genius" started getting used at two.

Now, at ten, she was long used to his high IQ and slightly quirky personality.

She didn't know where he got the brains—Sam Sutton hadn't exactly been a Mensa candidate, unless making and breaking promises gave a person more IQ points. Didn't matter. She was happy her boy had that advantage in life.

Except when it worked against him.

Right now, he was reading the schedule she'd printed and folded into thirds, his finger moving line by line as if he could memorize the whole week before they hit the parking lot.

"Name recognition, sit, down, leash manners. Vet talk on Day Three. Agility play. Please." He rolled his eyes with the skill of a teenaged girl. "We will conquer that the first morning."

"No need to overachieve, Ben."

"Wait. Socialization blocks." He hesitated there, the word landing heavy and awkward in the warm car. "Socialization? With dogs or kids?"

"Dogs need friends, too." She glanced in the mirror again. "Just like you. I bet you meet nice kids here."

"I'm focused on Sir Isaac Newton today," Benny said, in that practical, matter-of-fact tone he used when he wanted to get his way. "We should clarify the list of commands we want to be consistent with at home. I read that 'sit' versus 'sit down' can be confusing. Also, we need to pick a release word. 'Okay' is too common. The trainer in the video says 'free.' I like 'release.' It sounds official."

"It certainly does," she agreed, turning past a woodcut sign at the entrance of Canine Canyon Refuge.

She'd been here just before Christmas with her mother to pick up Sir Isaac Newton, and dear MJ had been so enamored with the doggies that Snowberry Lodge almost got one to entertain the guests.

The refuge was a multi-building campus tucked on the edge of town, a sweet place that cared for dogs and cats, despite the name. Also some insanely adorable goats.

She pulled into the lot and found a spot near the main building, eyeing the blue clapboard structure. A banner hung over the front door with bold lettering that said, "Welcome to Paws & Pals Winter Training Camp!"

To the right, a low barn hugged a paddock where a few goats nosed the snow curiously. Farther back, a small outbuilding held a cat "porch" with carpeted shelves pressed against a window. The whole place felt well-loved, painted in cheerful colors that made the day glow warmer.

"Mom," Benny said, voice soft in the back seat. "He's quivering."

"Puppy shivers," she answered, unbuckling. "It's excitement. And a little cold." She met Benny's eyes. "I get it."

He nodded, then bent to press his nose to Sir Isaac

Newton's head. "You're going to be excellent," he whispered to the dog. "Top of your class. Valedictorian."

Gracie's heart gave a small leap. How many times could you fall in love with your own child? Apparently, many. She climbed out, had a little shiver herself, then slid open the back door for Benny and...Sir Isaac Newton.

Did she really have to call him by a five-syllable name? Yes, according to his master. She hoped the other kids at camp would follow Benny's rules. If they didn't, she hoped he could like them anyway.

After all, this little sojourn had a bigger purpose than training the dog how to do what doggies did. As she and Nicole had discussed yesterday, this was part of Gracie's relentless campaign for Benny to make friends.

Benny unbuckled Sir Isaac Newton with careful fingers and anchored the leash, then slid out, putting the dog on the ground and laughing when he scampered on the snow.

On the walk toward the main building, Gracie held Benny's hand, and he held the leash to tug a not-so-sure Newt—don't tell Benny—toward training camp.

"Come on, boy," he urged gently. "We're going to camp together!"

He sounded so excited, her heart felt like it was folding in half. Benny needed a friend so badly and not just one with four legs.

He only had Red, his octogenarian great-grandfather. No friends, and no real father figure, she reminded herself for the guilt-ridden zillionth time.

"Hey," she said, holding the door with her boot while Benny managed the leash. "There will be lots of kids."

"I know."

"You can make friends."

"Don't need them," he said without hesitation. "I have Sir Isaac Newton." He slid her a look from behind his glasses, and then looked away, squaring his tiny shoulders as if to say, "Let me do it my way."

Yes, she was a famously overprotective mother, but she was alone in this journey and Benny was her whole world. Was that why he didn't make friends?

No, he simply liked his own company over anyone else's.

The front lobby of Canine Canyon was clean and bright, with the lingering scent of oatmeal shampoo. A chalkboard on one wall listed *Today's Camp Schedule* with hand-drawn paw prints walking between time slots.

A Christmas tree twinkled in the corner—small, with paper ornaments cut in the shapes of dog bones and snowflakes.

At the reception counter, a woman in a red fleece vest looked up from a tablet and smiled.

"Paws & Pals? Welcome!" Her gaze dropped to the dog. "And who is this handsome gentleman?"

"Sir Isaac Newton," Benny said, adjusting the leash like he'd practiced in the house last night.

"Oooh." She half laughed and looked at Gracie. "We've got royalty in the house."

Gracie smiled and looked down at Benny, who wasn't sure how to respond.

"And you are…"

"Benedict McBride," he said, the use of his full first name touching Gracie in ways she couldn't explain. "You can call me Benny."

"Hi, Benny. I'm Renee." She slid two laminated name tags across the counter—one for a human, one for a dog's collar—and a clipboard she gave to Gracie to complete. "First day is always a little noisy. Organized chaos. We get to the organized part by the end of the week, I promise."

The door opened behind them, ushering in a chilly blast of air and a father-daughter duo led by a gorgeous brindle dog with arresting blue eyes.

"Kat! Stop and heel, please." The little girl, who looked to be about Benny's age, shot the command with authority.

"Did she say *cat*?" Benny whispered, fighting a laugh.

The girl fired a look at Benny as she pulled a treat out of her pocket and gave it to her dog with praise.

"It's Kat with a K," she said, flipping one of many beautiful braids over her shoulder. "She's named for Katherine Johnson."

Benny stood a little straighter. "My dog's named Sir Isaac Newton, a famous physicist. Who's Katherine Johnson?"

"Never heard of Katherine Johnson?" Her brows shot up, espresso eyes flashing with disbelief. "Then maybe you need to read a little more."

Benny's jaw dropped. "I read a hundred books in the Scholastic Book Challenge last year."

"But you didn't read *Hidden Figures* or *Counting the Stars*, or you would know that Katherine Johnson was the first Black woman NASA mathematician whose critical calculations helped ensure the success of the Mercury-Atlas 6 orbit around the Earth."

Whoa. Gracie took a step backward and bumped right into the child's father, a tall and broad-chested man who sidestepped gracefully.

"I'm sorry," she muttered. "I just...wasn't expecting that."

The man chuckled, sliding his hands into the pockets of his khakis with a sigh that said nothing his daughter did surprised him. "Introduce yourself, Olivia. And Kat."

She put her hand on the dog's head. "This is Kat, a border collie, as you can probably tell by how she follows orders. They're smart. And I'm Olivia Hampton."

"Who makes the rules," the man next to Gracie whispered with a sly smile. "And enforces them."

Gracie laughed softly, taking a look at the stunning little girl who stood with perfect posture and maturity well beyond her nine or ten years.

"I'm Benny McBride," her son responded, his own back stiffening a little. "This is Sir Isaac Newton, a Cavapoo. He's part poodle, and they're smart, too."

Olivia looked dubious. "Does he have a nickname?"

"No. We use his whole name."

"My dog has a nickname."

"Which is also the name of another species," Benny reminded her.

"Species, yes. But still part of the animal kingdom,

chordate phylum, and mammal class," she fired back, crossing her arms. "Plus, it's super cute and funny."

"Oh, my..." Gracie turned to look up at Olivia's father, biting her lip. "I think my son just met his match."

"I'll pray for him," he said with another soft laugh, his eyes—the same midnight color as his daughter's—twinkling. "Because he'll need it."

"Can your dog sit and stay?" Olivia asked.

Benny blinked. "I just got him yesterday."

"Well, no treats, then." She stroked her dog's head. "Kat learned that in a day."

Just then, a couple came in with a little boy and a golden retriever puppy whose tail thumped the desk like a drumroll as the three dogs circled and barked.

Through it all, Renee managed to keep order, get names, and talk over the noise.

"Let's go, kids," she finally called out. "Camp starts in five minutes!"

Gracie gave Benny a hug and pressed her lips against his hair. "Be nice and make friends," she whispered.

"Do you think that dog is smarter than Sir Isaac Newton?"

"I don't know, but his owner seems pretty bright."

His eyes shuttered. "I didn't think my dog would have real competition."

"Benny." She crouched down, putting her hands on his shoulders. "She can be your friend."

He drew back, as aghast as a ten-year-old knew how to look. "She's right. Border collies are smart. She could win."

She exhaled and hugged him again. "There's nothing to win. It's not a competition."

"Yes, it is." He pointed to the bottom of the week's schedule to the words *Doggie Talent Show – Best Trick Wins Treats for a Year!*

Oh, boy. "Just have fun, Benny."

"Leash your dogs and follow me!" Renee stood in the doorway and waved the kids into a hall. "Parents, your work is done here. Say your goodbyes. Next time you see them, their dogs will come when called by name."

Gracie watched Benny and Sir Isaac head down the hall, keeping their distance from the adorable competition.

"Don't worry, she doesn't bite," Olivia's father said from just behind her. "Neither does the dog named Kat."

Laughing, Gracie turned and looked up at him. "I was hoping he'd make a friend as much as train the dog."

"He'll be fine. Kids and dogs. What could go wrong?"

She laughed again, then glanced toward the now empty hallway.

"Come on," he said, surprising her by gesturing toward the door. "You can see the training room from the windows that face the parking lot. I already scoped it out so I could surreptitiously keep an eye on her."

"Your daughter doesn't seem to need supervision," Gracie said, walking with him, aware of the sheer size of the man, who had to be six-two, with well-defined muscles under a thermal shirt and down vest.

"That doesn't stop me from hovering," he said, leading the way toward a bank of windows at the side of the building. "But I'm a single father, so I get to hover. I'm Marshall Hampton, by the way."

"Gracie McBride." He was a single dad? She should tell him she was in the parenting game alone, too. She should—

"Oh, look," he said, jutting his chin toward the windows to take in the chaos in the training room.

A dozen—maybe fourteen—kids clustered near the center, dogs tangling leashes and brushing noses. Staffers in matching blue shirts moved among them, cheerful and competent. A teenage volunteer collected coats and hung them. The floor was padded, a soft gray fleck that would be easy on paws and knees alike.

Gracie found Benny immediately. He was standing apart from the crowd, holding his dog in his arms, scanning the room—or sizing up the competition.

Olivia, on the other hand, was right in the middle, firing orders to Kat, who was in a bark-off with the golden retriever and completely ignoring her owner.

"I hope she can handle the chaos," Marshall said, his gaze on his daughter with a soft look of love. "You want your son to socialize and I want my daughter to learn that she can't control life with brains and determination. Sometimes, life controls you."

There was the tiniest note of sadness in his voice that made Gracie tear her attention from the training center to look up and study his profile.

He had strong features, rich dark skin, and long eyelashes. He turned and met her gaze, making her blink and look away so it didn't seem like she was staring at him.

"I hope they make friends with each other," he said. "Any kid who names his dog Sir Isaac Newton is definitely her kind of people."

"I hope they do, too."

After a moment, they stepped away and started walking back to the parking lot. There was a beat of awkward silence that Gracie so wanted to fill, but she didn't know what to say.

Poor Benny. He came by his struggles naturally.

"Do you have the week free before the New Year?" Marshall asked, obviously more skilled at small talk than she was.

"Oh, no," she said, grateful for something easy to talk about. "It's a busy season in my business."

"What do you..." His voice trailed off as she stopped next to her van. "Sugarfall? The bakery? Do you work there?"

"Actually, I own it."

His brows shot up and he slowed his step, looking at her with...respect? Awe? Worry? She wasn't sure.

"Have you been in?" she asked. "I'm in the back so much..."

"I've stopped by in moments of weakness," he admitted, sliding her a look. "Those cream puffs are deadly, so I usually just walk across the street."

Gracie felt her cheeks warm. "Deadly? I'm not sure I'd go that far, but you be careful on the other side of that street. I saw there's some construction starting in January. Something going up in the neighborhood."

"Yes," he said. "I've heard—" He pulled out a cell phone and glanced at it. "Sorry, better take this. And I'm over there." With his other hand, he pointed a key fob that flashed the lights on a muscular black truck. "I'm sure I'll see you around this week, Gracie."

She gave a smile and unlocked the van. As she climbed in, she pulled on the seatbelt and sighed, unsettled for reasons she didn't even understand.

Would Benny make friends? Would the bright little girl with the superstar dog intimidate or upset him? And *why* was Gracie so nervous, especially when it came to talking to a man?

Well, she'd always been timid, she reminded herself. She'd outgrown abject shyness in her late teens, but she'd never been bold or talkative or flirtatious. And as far as men?

The one and only time she'd fallen in love, it had been a colossal mistake.

Sam Sutton had been her "moment of weakness," to borrow the phrase that Marshall had just used, and twenty-four-year-old Gracie was sure she'd met "the one."

But when she accidentally got pregnant, Sam showed his true colors. He did *not* want a wife, or child, or house with a picket fence in Park City. He'd freaked out, bolted to Vegas with some friends, and soon announced that he got a job in a casino and was staying there.

That was more than ten years ago.

Sam had been in Benny's life from a distance. He sent the occasional Venmo, visited about once every year or two, made exactly one little league game, two Christmases, and zero school events.

Benny called him "Dad" but never knew him enough to really miss him. Her own father could have stepped into the role of a "man" in Benny's life, but George McBride had passed away when Benny was in kindergarten. Thankfully, there was Red—Benny's best pal on Earth.

And, oddly enough, that relationship worked very well. Maybe too well, since her grandfather managed to fill the hole in Benny's life.

She glanced into the rearview mirror just as Marshall's truck passed, giving her a glimpse of the handsome man at the wheel. He glanced her way and gave a smile and raised his hand.

What would it do to Benny if she were to...date? Ugh, she could barely bring herself to think the word.

But would it be good if she brought a man into his life? Maybe...a man who already had a child, knew how to love, and understood the challenges of being a single parent? A man like...

She peered in the direction the truck had gone, cringing at the memory of warning him to be careful around the construction like he was Benny's age. That was dumb, and he took off a second later.

She had no idea how to flirt or send signals to a man. Quiet by nature, she simply wasn't...sparkling.

But her baking was. So, maybe she could start with...a *deadly* cream puff.

Smiling at that, she headed to the bakery to make a few.

Chapter Four
Nicole

"So, wait—are you saying your parents just...got back together? After ten years? This week?" Cameron's voice carried a mix of incredulity and amusement as he nudged open the paper cup lid for a sip.

"Crazy, right?" Nicole couldn't keep the smile off her face as the two of them meandered along Park City's Main Street, soaking up the explosion of Christmas and all things winter and Western. "They divorced when I was eighteen, and it wasn't pretty. But then Dad came back to help at the lodge this Christmas, and...they just clicked again. Like all that lost time didn't matter."

She sipped her hot chocolate, taken in travel cups from Sugarfall. She'd been disappointed that Gracie was out getting Benny at camp when they'd met up there, but she'd introduce him to her cousin later.

Now, she just enjoyed Cameron's reaction to the story she'd shared when he asked about her family and where she'd grown up. She enjoyed everything about him, to be honest.

For one thing, he looked maddeningly good in black jeans, a soft flannel shirt under a fleece jacket, and a knit cap over dark blond hair. He radiated easy confidence, the kind that made her feel both flustered and flattered just to be walking next to him.

"That's...wow," Cameron said, shaking his head with a laugh. "That doesn't happen in real life. That's like a movie."

"It really is." Nicole adjusted the gray knit beanie over her ears, and shifted the cardboard cup of hot chocolate from one hand to the other. They paused in front of an art boutique, glancing at Tiffany-style lampshades in the windows, created by a Park City artist.

"What about your family?" she asked. "Local?"

"Heber," he said, referring to a town about half an hour away. "I live there, too," he said. "In fact, I live in a small house on my parents' property, so if that's an issue, run now."

She laughed. "Not an issue. My mom and I live in the same townhouse complex, only she owns hers and I'm renting with Bri, my roommate."

"The phone number-giver," he added with a grin.

"Do your parents ski, too?" she asked.

He hesitated, then shook his head. "Not as much as they used to. Right now they're on a cruise ship on the way to Ensenada, Mexico. Their one big getaway every year."

"Nice."

He nodded, threading them through some tourists coming out of a boutique. She glanced at the window, and caught her own reflection with his, getting a little shiver of satisfaction. They made a nice couple, she had to admit.

They walked on, pausing at a beloved book store, then a jeweler that filled a window with sparkling diamonds.

"So, how did you end up doing ski patrol?" she asked. "Was that always the dream job?"

He thought about it for a minute, an expression passing over his face that she couldn't quite read. "Well, I've been skiing since I was little, but I tried the nine-to-five thing after college—I worked in a mortgage company, if you can believe that."

She laughed. "Not in character at all."

"Amen. I wanted to crawl out of my skin, so I took the EMT basic training and honed my ski skills even more, and got the job, which I've had for about six years. In the off-season, I'm a firefighter for Summit County."

She drew back, slowing her step.

"What?" he scoffed at her surprised reaction. "You thought I was a total party animal ski bum who probably did mountain bike tours in the summer."

She laughed. "I admit...I wasn't expecting a firefighter. It's so...heroic."

That expression crossed his face again, but disappeared when he smiled and pinned those achingly blue eyes on her. "Don't be fooled," he said, slightly haltingly. "Not a hero."

"A firefighter and EMT?"

"Basic EMT. Not that impressive in the world of first responders. But I am midway through paramedic training, which is about two thousand hours of schooling. That'll really help on the slopes because paramedics' pay is well above mine. Now, I just stabilize and transport non-criticals."

"And as a firefighter?" she asked. "What do you do?"

"Fight fires," he joked. "Well, they use me as an EMT a lot, but I'm on the engine crew, standard shifts. I'm only on duty in the summer and fall when the wildfires are an issue, and when I'm not doing that, I'm in school, or taking care of...you know, life."

She studied him, completely shifting her very wrong first impression. "I really did think you were a partying ski bum."

"Well, patrollers are known to like to party after shift, so it's a fair mistake. But I never really was like that. And now? I'm thirty, so...ouch."

He spotted an empty bench on the corner, brushed off and just waiting for them. Guiding her there, he glanced down. "What about you, Nicole?"

"Two more years until thirty, so no ouch."

He laughed. "I mean, what's your deal? You manage a ski shop, your dad's a legendary skier, and the only two times I've seen you on the slopes—they were bunny and you were down. What's, uh, wrong with this picture?"

She let out a noisy breath as they sat, crossing her suede boots in front of her. She never liked telling the story. It never got easier or funny or less like a genuine brush with death.

But with him? For one thing, he'd know exactly what she was talking about. For another, well...he was protective by nature, so she trusted him.

"You know, when your dad is Flying Jack Kessler, skiing is not a hobby. It's a biography," she started.

He smiled a little, a flicker she liked. "I did put that together."

"And when you're nine and you've inherited his speed and fearlessness and low center of gravity, along with...I'm quoting him now, 'fast twitch muscle dominance and trunk stability'—"

"You've got an Olympian in the making."

She laughed softly, having heard all of that so many times. "Not quite at nine, but the hopes were there. Except there was this tree well..." She looked hard at him. "And that nine-year-old went face down into suffocation and near death. After that, I was just one scared little girl who refused to put skis on until"—she closed her eyes—"last week."

"Oh, wow," he whispered. "That's...wow. I'm sorry."

She nodded, throat tightening. "There's really not that much more to the story than that," she said. "It was a bad, bad day. I was with my dad, getting the old Kessler push to go faster, farther, and off the well-groomed trail. I thought I was invincible."

"The biggest mistake on skis."

"No kidding." She swallowed, closing her eyes and seeing the white powder, the green trees, soaring on her skis until...she wasn't. "The minute I went under, it felt like the mountain was eating me alive, like a mouth closing over me."

He sat very still, listening and letting her continue.

"I panicked. I struggled. That makes it worse, you

know? You wriggle deeper. You try to scream, which is bad. And then you realize whatever breath is in your lungs will most likely be the last one you ever take."

His eyes shuttered as he took her hand. "How long?"

"Not very, but it felt like a year until Dad got to me. He says it was seconds. It seemed like forever. He dug and dug, found my face, cleared my mouth, flipped me, and I came up like a fish. Everyone was on me, shouting, so grateful, and I was...done. With skiing, not life." She looked down at her hands. "I couldn't get back on skis. Not that season. Not the next. And then it became a fact about me, like my brown eyes and dark hair. Nicole doesn't ski."

"Therapy?"

"No," she said, shaking her head. "My parents talked about it but I just...no. I didn't want to ski, but I didn't need counseling. Well, maybe I did, but I never had it."

"Tree wells are no joke," he said, full authority in that statement. "They're monsters that look like pillows. I've pulled probably seven people out. I've seen someone..." He just shook his head and she knew exactly what he was going to say.

He'd seen someone die. Because it happened, just not to Nicole.

"I'm really glad you came back out," Cameron said finally. "Because the world wouldn't be as nice a place without you."

She smiled at the compliment, turning to him, wanting to be deeply honest, but not really understanding why.

"You know why I skied last week?" she asked. "I made a deal with my dad when I went to see him in Vermont over Thanksgiving weekend. If he'd come back and run our sleigh rides, I'd ski with him again. He did—and reunited with my mom—which was kind of my secret dream."

"It worked," he said. "And you skied."

"I wouldn't go that far. I put on skis and fell on my backside twice—which I expected but it's okay. I did it and my dad was happy."

"And you went again with Bri, right?"

She nodded. "I thought maybe I'd do better without Flying Jack. But I just wiped out."

"Would you go again?" he asked, his voice just gentle enough make her heart do silly things.

She didn't answer right away, but held his beautiful blue gaze.

"I did a back-country run a week ago," she said. "After my horse went down a slope at our lodge and I needed to get him."

He drew back, impressed. "You did? And you have a horse?"

She nodded. "It was a breakthrough, though. A big one."

"Enough that you'd go to Deer Valley with me tomorrow?"

She nodded slowly, not committing but clearly on her way.

"You can't be much safer than with a patrol," he added, as if she needed a push. "I know the very most gentle runs at DV, I know how to pace a beginner, and I..." He smiled. "I'd really like to ski with you, Nicole."

Realizing that they were still holding gloved hands, she squeezed his fingers. "You know what, Cameron? I will go with you. If you promise to take care of me."

"I promise." He looked right into her eyes and she melted like all this snow in the sun. "We can go down—" He frowned and fished out his phone, mumbling an apology as he looked at the screen. "I gotta take this. Hang on."

He stood, biting off his glove to tap the phone and put it to his ear, stepping a few feet away. "What's up?"

She looked ahead, not wanting to eavesdrop.

But he stayed close enough that she could catch the unmistakable lilt of a woman's voice on the other end.

Cameron's voice dropped, almost a murmur. She caught fragments and a sense of concern. "...yeah, I know...soon..." and then, more clearly, "...I'd better come back, just to be safe. No, no, it's fine."

He returned a minute later, stuffing the phone into his pocket. His easy grin was gone, replaced by tension. "I'm really sorry, but I've got to go."

Nicole blinked. "Oh. Is everything okay?"

"Yeah, but, uh, something came up." He was already half-turned, seeming restless. "I'll see you tomorrow? Meet at base around eleven or twelve? I'm not working but I'll be there. Just show up and we'll take a few runs."

So, it wasn't another date. And he was ditching her for...whoever just called.

"Uh...sure," she said, the response just as vague.

"Sorry! Bye!" With a quick wave, he jogged down the sidewalk, disappearing into the crowd before Nicole could gather her thoughts.

She stared after him, hot chocolate cooling in her hands. *What just happened?*

Pulling her jacket tighter, she stood and started back toward Sugarfall. Maybe Gracie would be back by now.

Nicole needed her cousin's voice of reason—someone to tell her whether she'd just imagined the chemistry, or whether Cameron was too good to be true, and what to do when one got dumped in the middle of a first date.

NICOLE SLIPPED into Sugarfall by way of the back door, getting hit by the warmth of the kitchen and a rush of butter and vanilla and heat. Gracie stood at the far counter with her sleeves pushed to her elbows, coaxing glossy ribbons of white over a tray of her famous cream puffs.

She glanced up, her golden brown eyes widening, her strawberry blond hair pulled back in a tight pony tail.

"What are you doing here, Nic? Aren't you supposed to be on a date? I was hoping it would go through dinner."

Nicole made a face that probably needed no translation.

"Oh, no. What happened? Hang on. You deserve one of these." She grabbed two of the prettiest pastries and swept them onto a plate. "Come on."

They wove out to the front, where the bakery patrons had thinned to an afternoon lull. Nicole followed her cousin across the black-and-white checked floor to a two-top by the window.

Gracie wiped it, and set down the plate. "I'll grab napkins and—what are we feeling? Coffee? Tea? Something stronger that I'm not licensed to serve?"

"A tea, I guess," she said glumly. "I just had hot chocolate."

Gracie returned with two thick mugs, strings from the bags hanging out the side. She sat and angled her chair toward Nicole, all attention. "Okay. Talk."

Nicole looked around. "You didn't bring Benny back here after camp? How was it?"

"He's home with Red. It was good, I guess."

"Did he make a friend?" Nicole asked.

Gracie rolled her eyes. "Quite the opposite. A darling little girl who just might be smarter than Benny is threatening to win the end-of-camp talent show where each kid shows off tricks that their dog learned. So he doesn't have a friend, but a sworn enemy."

"Oh, no." Nicole pressed her hands to her cheeks. "That's not what we wanted."

Gracie smiled, waving off the problem. "Forget camp. How was your date and why is it over already? Didn't you guys meet here like an hour or two ago?"

Nicole nodded, eyeing the cream puff, but not hungry. "The 'date,' if you could call it that, was amazing. That's the problem."

Gracie gave a confused look. "'Kay. Elaborate."

She did, sharing the whole date—such as it was. As expected, Gracie listened intently without a single interruption, a trait she dearly loved in her cousin. After she finished, Nicole looked down at the cream puff, but only saw the look in Cameron's eyes when he took off and left her on a park bench.

"So, he just...disappeared?" Gracie asked, processing it all.

Nicole broke off a piece of the pastry, watching Gracie's signature cream ooze out, but she really had no appetite.

"I wasn't trying to eavesdrop, but I have ears—there was definitely a woman's voice on that call."

"It must have been work," Gracie said. "Patrol gets called in last-minute, right?"

"Why not tell me that?"

"Maybe his mother needed him and he was embarrassed to admit he runs when she calls?"

Nicole laughed. "Not likely, since his mother is on a cruise to Mexico."

"Oh. Well..." Gracie frowned, thinking. "He's a firefighter. Maybe there was an emergency."

"He only works summer and fall, but even if that were true, why not just tell me that? I'd have understood."

Gracie shook her head, as stumped as Nicole. "Well, eat that. You'll feel better. Although..." She chuckled. "I was told today by a very handsome man that they are 'deadly.'"

Nicole took a bite and moaned. "Then this is how I

want to go."

As she ate, Gracie looked around the bakery thought-fully. "Maybe he was nervous around you."

Nicole nearly choked on her cream puff. "Try again."

"I'm serious. Take it from an introvert. Nerves scramble brains. People say the wrong thing or forget common courtesies. Don't write him off because of one confusing exit."

"The man saves lives, skis fearlessly, and probably doesn't know the meaning of the word nervous." Nicole took a lick of cream that actually should be illegal just as her phone buzzed in the pocket of her jacket, a tiny, trai-torous leap of hope jumping inside her.

She pulled it out and stared at the screen.

"Oh."

"What?" Gracie leaned, looking down.

"It's him. He wrote, 'I'm sorry for leaving so fast. That was not my style, I swear. Got called in to an almost emergency, but all is well. Ski tomorrow?'" She sighed, surprised at how relieved the text made her.

Gracie looked smug. "Told ya."

"What's an 'almost' emergency?" Nicole asked.

"Just accept his apology and give him another chance, Nic."

"And ski?" She lifted both brows because Gracie knew how much that terrified her, even though she'd made huge progress the past few weeks.

"You did it to save Copper," Gracie reminded her. "This time do it for you. He'll take care of you."

She knew that was true, so she typed back her

response to Cameron without giving herself too much time to think about it.

Glad everything's okay. Yes to tomorrow. She added a ski emoji, which was probably dorky, but so was dumping her in the middle of their date.

"You're doing it?" Gracie asked, delighted. "Way to go!"

"I'm giving him—and the slopes—a shot," Nicole said as she hit Send. Then, because her heart needed a different subject, she tipped her head. "How handsome?"

"Excuse me?"

Nicole grinned around her next bite. "The guy who called these deadly. You said he was handsome."

"Did I?" Her color deepened around her sweet smattering of freckles, which wasn't unusual. Gracie blushed as easily as she breathed.

"Yes. Tell me about him," Nicole demanded.

"Oh, nothing to tell," she said.

Nicole finished the last bite and dabbed at her lips with a napkin, eyeing her cousin. "Why don't *you* date?"

"Date?" Gracie scoffed, maybe a little too hard.

"Yeah. You're so quick to tell me to give Cameron a chance and ski, of all insane things, but I never hear you talk about anyone."

"Because I'm a single mom of a ten-year-old, Nic. And I'm married to my business. Also, I live with my geriatric grandfather. Can you imagine if I invited someone in for a nightcap? They'd end up playing Monopoly with Red."

Nicole snorted. "Not only would they lose, they'd be

subjected to his opinions on everything. But,"—she pointed at Gracie—"there are worse ways to spend an evening and the right guy would know that."

Gracie shrugged, her dark amber gaze distant as she looked away.

"Why not?" Nicole pressed. "I mean, if I can ski, you can date."

She shook her head. "I have a kid who needs me and a business that consumes me, and by the end of the day I want pajamas and the *Great British Baking Show*, not a meet-cute. I mean, I could, but I'd rather not."

"Do you know who you sound like?"

"Someone who knows what they want?"

"You sound exactly like Benny when you ask him to make friends. 'I could but I'd rather not,'" Nicole mimicked Benny perfectly.

Gracie cracked up. "Well, that's humbling. And so true I could scream. Genes are strong, I guess."

"If you want him to make a friend that much, maybe he feels the same way about you having a man in your life."

"He's *ten*," Gracie insisted.

"He's *Benny*," Nicole shot back. "Ten going on fifty-three with a brain that works overtime. Don't you think his feelings are as advanced as his IQ? Don't you think he'd love a role model who wasn't born during World War Two?"

"Of course I do," Gracie admitted with a sigh. "The deadly guy? He was another parent at camp."

"Oh, so married."

She smiled. "Actually, he referred to himself as a single dad."

"Mmm? Hopeful. More details, please."

"His name is Marshall with a little spitfire of a daughter who gave Benny a run for his money in the brains and 'tude department, and he likes my cream puffs."

Nicole raised a brow. "Are you sure that's not a euphemism for something else?"

Gracie chuckled. "He saw the logo on my van and they usually are the first thing everyone mentions. They're not nearly as good as my Linzer tarts, but cream puffs get all the PR."

"So, he's single, cute, and has good taste in pastries. What are you waiting for?"

"Um...Benny to go to college?" she said on a laugh. "No, seriously, I'm not the outgoing person you are, Nic. And this guy was a tad out of my league, if I'm being honest."

"Out of your *league*?" Nicole drew back. "Are you kidding? You are gorgeous and own this amazing business and are the best mother. He'd be so lucky to take you out." Nicole reached across the table and squeezed her hand. "I'm serious."

"Thanks." Gracie looked around again. "Maybe I'll take him a cream puff at the end of camp."

"Or tomorrow."

"Don't rush me." Gracie smiled as Nicole's phone buzzed again. "Is that him?"

She glanced down. "Yep. He says, 'Promise I'll

explain tomorrow. Wasn't trying to be rude. Can't wait to tackle every double black D. JK!'"

Gracie pointed at her. "I *like* a man with a sense of humor," she said. "Plus, he obviously is telling you he respects your fears and he's wallowing in guilt for what he did."

"You got *all* that out of one text?"

Gracie laughed. "So, you're going skiing with a cute boy."

"How do you know he's cute?"

"I blush, but you glow." She winked. "I want every detail afterwards."

"You'll get them," Nicole promised, leaning in. "*If* you ask the single dad on a date."

"Me? Ask him? Are you kidding?"

"Hey, I'm going on a ski date," she reminded Gracie. "If I can do that, then you can at least give a man a cream puff and throw your phone number in the box."

"He knows where to find me."

Nicole leaned in, knowing her always reticent cousin often needed a good push down the slopes of life. "What's the worst that could happen?"

Gracie gave the saddest smile. "I fall in love, get my heart smashed, and you have to pick up the pieces. *Again.*"

"I was only eighteen when you went through that with Sam," Nicole said, remembering the dark days after her cousin's unexpected pregnancy and subsequent heartbreak.

"You were there for me, though, even though your

own parents were getting a divorce and you were starting college." Gracie reached over the table and put her hand on Nicole's. "I don't know where I'd be without you, Nic."

Touched, Nicole squeezed her hand, then grinned. "I do love irony," she said. "We send Benny to camp to find a friend...and you meet your one true love?"

Gracie pushed back to stand. "Girl, you watch too many rom-coms and I have to go bake."

"Make an extra cream puff."

"I will," Gracie said with a smile. "And let's hope we don't both wipe out."

"Amen to that, sweet cuz."

Chapter Five
MJ

MJ slipped into her small suite of rooms as the lovely late afternoon settled over Snowberry Lodge. With her two full-time employees taking the week off, today had been a bear. Not only was the lodge at capacity, she'd had two check-outs followed by two check-ins, countless food requests, the occasional emergency, and they were still in full Christmas mode.

Her sister decided to end the day with another snowmobile ride with Jack, but MJ just wanted to rest.

She slipped into her comfy chair, feet up on the ottoman, head back, happy to be in the little corner of the world that she called home. Technically, she "lived" at Starling House with her Gracie, Benny, and Red. At least, she had a room there and many of her belongings.

But she hadn't slept there since George died. The empty bed in their old room was just too lonely.

So, she'd migrated to this sizeable suite right off the kitchen. It only made sense to stay here. She often rose at five A.M. to get breakfasts going and once in a while, a guest needed something in the middle of the night. George used to trudge down to the lodge when that happened, but with him gone and Cindy living fifteen minutes away at her townhouse, MJ had to step in.

So this was her home now, and that was just fine.

Just as she got comfy, she heard footsteps in the kitchen and held her breath, hoping they weren't followed by the ding of the small bell she kept on the counter for guests to contact her. They were welcome to the fridge and pantry, but sometimes they needed—

She almost grunted at the sound of the bell.

They needed her.

Pushing up, she smoothed out her slacks and straightened her sweater, stepping out to see a man in a ski jacket, gloves dangling from the zipper. "I hate to bother you, but we have a problem," he announced.

"How can I help you, Mr. Kingsley?" she asked, grateful that she hadn't lost her keen eye and the skill that allowed her to remember every guest's face and name. "The kitchen's always open."

"That's kind of you, but we're actually headed out into Park City for the evening, but we, uh, noticed a leak in the bathroom. Toilet keeps running and there's water on the bathroom floor." He cringed in apology. "I'd hate to see it cause any damage."

And so would she. MJ's heart dropped, knowing exactly which bathroom he meant, in one of their largest rooms called the Aspen Suite, directly over the dining area. And the Kingsley family of four couldn't easily be moved to another room—not that the Snowberry Lodge had a single vacancy right now.

That was a good problem to have. A leaky toilet? Not so much.

"We'll get it all fixed up while you're gone," she assured him cheerfully, despite the fact that an emergency evening plumber would not be easy to find the day after Christmas. "You don't mind if someone enters your suite?"

"Not if you don't care that my kids' suitcases look like bombs went off."

She just laughed. "Not a bit. Thank you for letting me know. Have a wonderful time in Park City."

When he left, MJ exhaled. Of course this happened while Pedro was on vacation. Should she call Red? Her dad knew his way around a plumbing problem, but he'd looked so tired when he stopped in this morning, she didn't want to bother him.

First, she'd assess how bad it was, she decided, heading to the mudroom for her toolbox.

In the coat closet, she reached for the red metal case that had gotten her through a few such emergencies. The thing weighed a ton and she couldn't carry it upstairs, but she dragged it out, flipped it open, and crouched down to get the tools she might need without hauling the monster up the stairs.

The back door clicked and creaked and she looked up, a wrench in one hand, a screwdriver in the other.

"Looks like you're about to do battle." Matt stepped inside, mostly in silhouette with the waning light behind him. He wasn't in his usual lodge-casual flannel but a trim, olive-green sweater over a collared shirt and dark slacks.

"Just part of the glamour of lodge ownership," she said, pushing to a stand, grateful for the hand he offered to help her up. "A leaky toilet waits for no woman."

He chuckled, a warm, rolling sound that she'd gotten quite used to hearing.

"Are you on your own today? No Jack? Pedro? Red?"

"Jack is out on that snowmobile you gave us." She slipped into a huge smile. "Unless I dreamed that."

"Nope. Real deal."

She just shook her head, the very idea of it still leaving her speechless. "Pedro and Nina have the week off, Red's at home, and I..." She wiggled the wrench. "Am tackling toilets."

With a chuckle, he reached over, flipped the toolbox closed and snapped the latches. In one smooth move, he scooped it up by the handle.

"Which room?"

She drew back. "Oh, I couldn't let you—"

"You think you can beat that toilet with kindness and a good attitude? If so, there's no one better than you. If not, I'm your man."

Her man? Her heart did something no sixty-two-year-old heart ought to do, but surely that was just because he was offering to help. Especially since he was staying in their most expensive cabin and wearing...Ralph Lauren.

"Thank you, Matt, but that optimism says I can find the problem. You're dressed for a nice dinner, not plumbing."

He glanced down. "Too much? I never know. Anyway, how do plumbers dress?"

"In overalls. Dirty T-shirts. Maybe a baseball cap over a bald head."

He looked a little wistful, as if he'd prefer overalls to Lauren. "Guess you've been around the wrong plumbers." Lifting the toolbox like it weighed nothing, he headed toward the door. "Show me the way, Mary Jane." At her surprised expression, he shrugged. "I heard Cindy call you that the other day. I like it. Really suits you, you know?"

Once again, her chest felt...unusual. But she had to remember all that she and Cindy and Jack had talked about last night. Yes, Cindy did sometimes playfully call her by her given name. Or had he...been researching how to con a widow?

"Which room?" he asked again.

"I'm sorry, Matt. I simply couldn't let you—"

He leaned an inch closer. "Would you feel better if I scared up a pair of work pants and boots? I am a plumber, MJ. Licensed, certified, and capable of fixing anything involving a toilet, pipe, or drain."

Her jaw dropped. "You are?"

"Yeah, and based on your image of the whole profession, I take it as a compliment that you're surprised. I'm retired, but plumbing isn't fast-moving technology, unless you have one of those ten-thousand-dollar Japanese toilets that run on an app. Has anything so stupid ever been invented?"

She laughed, remembering that before Cindy had

planted seeds of doubt, she'd thoroughly enjoyed this man's unique sense of humor.

"Does this look like a place that would have a ten-thousand-dollar toilet?" she countered.

He just smiled and led her out of the kitchen with the lightest touch on her back. "Bring the wrench. I guarantee we'll need it. And do you want to grab towels for the floor?"

A...plumber. A *plumber*? She processed that news as she reached up to the rag bin, grabbing a handful of cleaning towels. Then she walked him through the dining area, past the living room, and up the wide staircase to the second floor.

The whole time, she only had one thought: Matt Walker was a plumber. A charming, tanned, well-dressed, generous plumber.

Did that make her trust him more...or less? She'd heard they did well, but enough to afford an expensive cabin for weeks on end? Enough to gift near-strangers a costly snowmobile?

She wasn't sure if she believed him or not. Well, if he could fix a toilet, then maybe.

"I haven't been up to this part of the lodge," he said as they reached the top of the stairs. "It's spacious."

"This floor has five rooms, and there are three more downstairs," she told him. "One huge space in the attic, but we stopped using it a long time ago. And it's like any other older woman—don't look too close, you'll see the cracks and flaws."

"I remember you said this was originally your grandfather's house," he said, looking at the moldings and framed art as they walked down a wide hall, their feet soft on the Oriental runner that covered the plank floors.

"My grandparents, Owen and Irene Starling, ran this place as a horse farm and this was their original home. When Park City started shifting away from mining and the skiers discovered our amazing mountains, they turned this into an inn and built another smaller house on the property, where Cindy and I grew up."

"The history is beautiful," he mused.

"Snowberry Lodge is part of our family DNA," she said, tapping on the door at the end of the hall before bringing out the master key. "They've left to go into town, but warned me the kids are a bit messy."

She stepped in first, with Matt right behind her.

"Messy is an understatement," Matt joked as they walked into a room that looked like the kids had a war with their clothes. The king bed was made, and the parents had obviously made use of the dresser and closets.

But the young ones, who were using the bunks at the far end of the room, hadn't bothered putting their clothes away.

Still, the mess didn't detract from what was one of MJ's favorite suites in the lodge.

A corner room with a big bay window overlooking the tops of snow-draped pines, it offered a mountain view almost as breathtaking as the one Matt had in Cabin Five. This suite had a fireplace, too, and an en suite that featured a massive Jacuzzi-style tub. And a leaking toilet, it seemed.

"Nice," Matt said as they entered the bathroom.

"It is, but so outdated. And the floor is wet." She started laying the old towels she'd brought, gauging the damage, which wasn't much yet.

"I think we're nice and early," Matt said as he set down the toolbox and knelt on one of the towels in front of the toilet like he'd done it a hundred times. Which, apparently, he had.

"Running nonstop?" he asked.

She nodded, hovering near the vanity. "That's what the guest said."

He lifted the tank lid and peered inside. "Float valve's not sealing. Common problem." Without hesitation, he rolled up his sleeves.

"You don't mind, do you?" she asked again, feeling awkward.

"MJ, if you knew how many of these I've fixed in my life..." He started to plunge his hand into the cold water. "Whoops. Better take this off first."

He tugged at his wrist and snapped free a watch, reaching toward the sink, but the counter around it was wet and covered with their guests' belongings.

"Can you—"

"Of course." She took the watch from him, and the weight surprised her.

She glanced down and saw the word Rolex on the face, somehow just knowing this wasn't a knock-off or even like the ones George used to eye in the airport duty-free cases. He'd always joked about owning a Rolex, his sign for having "made it" in the world.

She'd looked into how much a Rolex cost, longing to buy him one for his fiftieth birthday. But she gave up that idea when she saw the price tags, which were astronomical.

But this plumber owned one, the kind with the blue face and tiny diamonds, too.

While he worked, she turned the watch in her hands, tracing the smooth links. Then her eyes caught the engraving on the back: *Graham Walker*, with a year—*this* year.

Graham. Not Matthew?

Her stomach twisted. This wasn't an old heirloom that belonged to his father, not with the current year engraved on it. Why would a plumber introduce himself under a different name? Why would a plumber own a watch that cost enough to buy a car? A luxury model.

Cindy's warnings echoed in her head.

People who want something don't always announce it. Sometimes they start by finding the heart and coming in that way. He already knows we're in financial trouble.

Matt's voice interrupted her spiraling thoughts. "Pass me that wrench?"

She startled, placed the watch carefully on some towels on the counter, and handed him the tool. He tightened something inside the tank, jiggled the float, and in a moment the incessant trickle stopped.

"Fixed," he announced with satisfaction.

"Just like that?"

"Just like that." He rose, rinsed his hands in the sink, and dried them on the guest towel like a man who belonged. Then he picked up the watch, sliding it back on his wrist with ease.

Her mind buzzed with questions. *Graham Walker? Why lie about your first name?*

"How can I ever thank you?" she asked lightly, praying he wouldn't hear the nervous edge.

His eyes warmed, then lit with something almost boyish. "Dinner."

She blinked. "Of course I'll make you dinner. Just name your favorite dish and I bet I can..." Her voice faded as he shook his head.

"I, uh, I actually meant I'd like to take you to a nice dinner in town, MJ," he said, the color in his cheeks telling her that was not easy for him to ask.

Her mouth opened, closed, opened again. Well, she had promised Cindy to find out more. What could be more natural than asking personal questions over dinner?

Which made it a *date*.

"That's...unexpected," she managed.

"I don't mean to presume," he said quickly, hands sliding into his pockets. "But I enjoy your company and if ever there was a woman who needed to relax in a nice restaurant, it's you."

She laughed despite herself. "That's true."

"And I saved you from toilet disaster."

"So I should be treating *you* to dinner," she countered.

"Having dinner with you would be my treat," he said.

People who want something don't always announce it. Sometimes they start by finding the heart and coming in that way.

She ignored the repeating voice in her head and looked up at him, searching his light brown eyes for any hint of subterfuge, finding nothing but kindness and warmth.

And a different name on his watch.

She *had* to find out more about him. "I'd like that, Matt," she said softly. "Thank you."

His smile lit the room. "Tomorrow night?"

"Tomorrow night," she echoed.

"Then let's finish drying this room, huh?" He looked down quickly, almost as if the exchange embarrassed him or...worried him?

She couldn't tell, but together they finished drying the floor, and he insisted on carrying the dirty towels and the toolbox, which he did with ease.

"I'm going to go change," he said after they'd finished putting everything away or in the laundry.

"Can I wash those..." She glanced at his expensive sweater.

"I have a dry cleaning pickup tomorrow," he told her. "It's all good. Mind if I choose the restaurant?"

She smiled. "Of course. But don't go over—"

He held up his hand. "Trust me."

With that, he gave a nod and headed back outside into the cold, leaving her standing there with his words reverberating as loudly as the washer she'd just started.

Trust me?

Could she? Maybe she'd find out tomorrow night.

Chapter Six
Gracie

Snow had fallen overnight, so Gracie was grateful her bakery van had all-wheel drive as she pulled out from Snowberry Lodge to take Benny to his second day of camp.

Benny was busy trying to hold Sir Isaac Newton, who thought the vehicle was his personal playground. From the console, the scent of coffee from her travel mug tempted her, mixing with the lingering sweetness from the cake she'd delivered yesterday.

"Sit, Sir Isaac Newton. Sit." Benny pushed at the dog's backside, but ol' Newt just tried to climb into the front, stopped by the short leash attached to the seatbelt buckle. "Come on, doggo! You have to start listening to my commands."

"He will do better at camp when you have treats for him."

"Too many treats aren't good for his liver," he told her with a voice of authority she rarely questioned. "I need a better way to make him listen. I did all the research last night—thank you for letting me use Grandpa's phone, by the way."

"Just follow the rules. Research only on approved

sites." She'd lost the battle to keep technology out of her little boy's hands. Now, it was supervised on Red's phone.

"I'm going to make him a whistle at forty thousand hertz," Benny continued. "I can do it, too, with some plastic tubing and a bottle cap. Grandpa said he'll help me."

She looked up into the rearview mirror, not sure she could follow that. "Forty thousand...what?"

"Dog whistles work because they produce ultrasonic frequencies that we can't hear, but dogs can. That's going to be my secret weapon at the contest."

"Secret...are you sure that's allowed?"

He laughed. "Nobody can hear but the dogs. And Sir Isaac Newton's whistle will be special because smaller dogs are more sensitive to slightly higher frequencies. I've got it all figured out, Mom."

She had no doubt he did. "Is that what you and Grandpa were working on last night? I heard a lot of laughter and maybe somebody jumping up and down. Please tell me that was you. Or the dog. Not my grandfather."

He snorted a laugh. "Grandpa slept mostly, which is what he always does."

"He's eighty-two, honey."

"Well, he's my best friend, so I wish he'd stay awake."

Her heart twisted. Yes, Red Starling was a fantastic great-grandfather to her son, but he should not be Benny's only friend. Despite asking him about friends at camp several times last night, Benny only talked about the dogs, the contest, and how awesome Sir Isaac Newton was. And how annoying Olivia Hampton was.

On a sigh, she adjusted the vent, fingers tightening around the wheel as she navigated the winding road that led toward Canine Canyon. The sky was pale gray, low clouds hanging like a lid over the mountains, which would be great for skiing, but not so much for driving back here this afternoon.

Her eyes flicked to the passenger seat. A small pink box with the Sugarfall logo sticker on top, closed over two delicious cream puffs she'd made before leaving work last night.

The question was, did she have the nerve to present them to tall, good-looking Marshall Hampton and maybe...suggest they get a coffee sometime?

She let out a soft grunt of nerves. Gracie was only confident when she was in the kitchen, elbow-deep in dough, or applying the delicate frosting artwork to a canvas of cake or pastry.

Asking a man out? Oh, that was so not in her wheelhouse.

Nicole was right. If Gracie didn't step out of her comfort zone and "make a friend," then how did she expect her son to do the same?

"Okay," she whispered to herself. "Today's the day."

She peeked in the rearview mirror. Benny stroked Sir Isaac Newton's fur, carefully adjusting a bandana made from fabric that glowed with neon rockets and cartoon planets—courtesy of MJ.

The pup gazed up at him with unshakable adoration

—blissfully unaware that Benny wanted to train him with...frequencies.

"I just don't know about the trick," Benny mused, his eyes narrowing behind his glasses as they did when he was in deep thought.

"I thought you were going to do something space-related," she said. "Have him circle you and call it 'orbiting' or something?"

He gave a wry snort that made him sound five times his age. "I was, but that Olivia girl is doing something space-related. She's doing one called 'blast off,' where her dog jumps after she says, 'Three, two, one.'" He made a face. "Why didn't I think of that?"

"Maybe you could work with her and come up with another idea."

He gave her an "are you kidding?" look. "Not a chance. She thinks she's all that and a bag of...kibble."

She bit back a laugh because he sounded so much like Red.

"She thinks she has some kind of special claim on space because of some movie. Like, she's going to hate this..." He flicked at the rocket-covered bandana. "It'll just make her mad."

Whoa. Was that the smart-kid equivalent of pulling her pigtails? Well, in Olivia's case, gorgeous professional braids.

"Oh, I forgot to tell you, Mom," he said suddenly. "Miss Renee said they need someone to deliver the treats to the dogs. I was thinking Grandpa could come as Santa.

He said he would but..." He started laughing to himself, like he was remembering an inside joke.

"But what?"

"Only if my trick is to hold Sir Isaac Newton over a soft cushion, drop him carefully, and say, 'There—he proved gravity.'" His shoulders moved as he cracked up, and Gracie did, too.

"That sounds like my grandfather." Then she snapped her fingers as a thought occurred to her. "But maybe he's on to something, Ben."

"What? I'm not going to drop my dog, Mom."

"No, but aren't there three famous Newtonian laws?"

He thought about it for exactly, well, a nanosecond. "Of course. Inertia. Force and acceleration. Action and reaction. Remember, I wrote my science report on them."

"Well, show those laws. You could—"

"Mom!" He clapped his hands once, his eyes flashing. "That's it! I could have him stay still for law one, go down that little play slide for law two, and stop a moving ball for law three."

Gracie felt her jaw drop, endlessly amazed by this delightful and brilliant little boy. "Yes, yes, and yes!"

"You're a genius, Mom!"

She just shook her head, knowing who the real genius in the family was.

He picked up the Cavapoo and they touched noses. "We're going to win, Sir Isaac Newton! We'll show that dumb dog named Kat."

"Benny." She purposely put a warning note in her voice. "Be nice. And don't say her dog is dumb."

"She's not, and that's the problem," he muttered. "The dog is so smart it's scary."

Before she could pursue that, her phone rang from her purse and the dashboard lit up with the caller's name: Sam Sutton.

It's about time, she thought glumly at the sight of Benny's father's name. Christmas was two days ago.

"It's Dad!" he said, leaning forward. "Aren't you going to answer? I want to tell him about Sir Isaac Newton!"

The dog Sam didn't know about because *he didn't call on Christmas Day* like a normal, reliable, decent father would.

Gracie swallowed hard and hit the speaker button. "Hey, Sam."

"Hi, Grace," Sam's voice came through, smooth and cheerful, like honey on glass. He never called her Gracie like every other person on the face of the earth. Always just "Grace," and she didn't know why, but it irked.

"Hey, Dad! Guess what?"

"And my man, Benny-boy! How's my champ?"

Benny practically unbuckled himself, leaning toward the dash as though he could crawl through the screen. "I got a puppy, Dad! Just like I told you I would."

"You did? That's awesome, bud."

"I had the best idea and turned Grandpa into 'Grumpy Santa' on TikTok and it went viral and we were able to fill the whole lodge for December and Aunt Cindy said if I did that, I'd get a puppy, which I did, but she didn't know it was me because I'm not allowed to use the phone yet but—"

"Whoa, whoa, *whoa*. Hold up there, big boy. Slow down and tell me like I'm five, because I'm confused by your brilliance."

Benny laughed, but Gracie just sighed. He was so excited to share his life with his distant dad, and all he got was the occasional call. Like this one, two days after Christmas.

Yes, Sam had his own family—a wife and three-year-old son in Las Vegas. Five years ago, he married a girl named Coco, of all the grating names, and then she had a baby and the calls grew so infrequent, sometimes Gracie forgot the man existed.

Maybe Benny did, too. He didn't say.

"Anyway, Dad, it's a long story," Benny said, "and we're pulling into the puppy training camp. I can't be late because I want my dog to lead the line to playtime. He's a natural leader, you should see. Of course, that *other* dog tries to muscle in."

"Aw, I wish you had more time to tell me about the dog," Sam said. "Really sorry I didn't call on Christmas. We were in Reno with Coco's parents—"

"The dog's name is Sir Isaac Newton," Gracie interrupted, her voice brisk and steel-edged. She wasn't about to let her son sit through a story about Sam's shiny new family and their lovely Christmas.

Sam let out a hearty laugh. "Of course it is. What kind of dog, kiddo?"

"Cavapoo," Benny said proudly. "That's a Cavalier King Charles Spaniel mixed with a poodle, which makes him really smart."

"As smart as you, big guy?"

The slathering of meaningless nicknames made Gracie flinch and clench the wheel tighter as she looked for a parking spot. Big guy, kiddo, buddy. It all felt so forced and fake, like Sam himself.

"And Mom just had the best idea for his trick! He's going to demonstrate Newton's three laws. Isn't that amazing?"

"She is...amazing."

Her eyes shuttered and she kept her lips sealed. Not "amazing" enough for Sam. Not amazing enough to marry and help raise a child.

"There's a contest, Dad," Benny prattled on. "Like a talent show at the end of camp. And if we win, which we will, I'll get a big trophy! It's on stage and there will be an audience, too."

"Cool," Sam said, almost sounding like he meant it. "I'd love to see it."

"You should come!" Benny exclaimed, making Gracie's stomach drop to the floorboards of the van.

"I could do that, buddy boy," Sam said. "I'll drive over for the day."

A seven hour drive? Sure, Sam.

"Really?" Benny squealed.

"Sam, it's on New Year's Eve day," Gracie said stiffly. "I doubt you'll be free."

"Well, uh..." He cleared his throat. "I'll make myself free. For Benny. And Sir Isaac Newton."

"Dad! That would be so cool!"

Wincing at the disappointment she already knew this would bring, she turned into a parking spot and looked at Benny's bright and excited face, knowing how that smile would disappear when Sam failed to show.

"I'll do it," Sam said. "I'll be there."

Or he'd have an excuse, an apology, and another empty promise that it would be different next time.

"Yay!" Benny shouted so loud, the dog jumped and barked.

"Oh, I hear Isaac!" Sam said on a laugh.

"He's excited to meet you," Benny said, not even correcting his father with the dog's full name like he did everyone else. And it was time to step in.

"That would be lovely, Sam," she said, keeping her voice even. "But we understand if you can't make it."

"I wouldn't miss it for the world," he gushed. "I was calling about making a visit, so this is perfect."

Her stomach churned. He *would* miss it. He always did.

"That would be so awesome, Dad," Benny crooned, glowing. "Because at the end, they're doing a special photo booth for Dads 'n' Dogs. We could take a picture together."

"Dads 'n' Dogs?" Gracie choked. He'd never mentioned that.

"Don't worry," Benny said quickly, probably seeing

her expression in the mirror. "There's one called Moms 'n' Mutts, so you'll get a picture, Mom."

"Dads 'n' Dogs?" Sam repeated, amused. "Sounds perfect. Count me in, champ."

Benny was smiling so hard it had to hurt his face.

And Gracie didn't want to say anything that would wipe that smile away.

"Well, we're at the dog refuge," she said, putting the van in Park. "So you two say your goodbyes and we won't hold you to—"

"I'll be there, Grace," he said, his voice lower. "I can come and I want to. I mean, assuming that's okay with you."

"Of course," she said, feigning brightness she certainly didn't feel. "I'll text you the time and place."

"Perfect. And Merry Christmas, you two."

They said their goodbyes, Benny still bubbling with excitement.

"So, why didn't you tell me about the photo thing, Benny?"

Benny shrugged, adjusting his glasses. "Because I knew it would make you sad."

The words sliced through her, clean and brutal. He said them so casually, as if managing her sadness was just another chore.

She blinked hard, turning to get her purse. Should she warn Benny not to count on his father showing that day? Would he even listen? Benny's hopefulness was stubborn and blind. Sometimes he was so much like her mother, MJ, the eternal optimist.

It had gotten Benny through plenty of letdowns where Sam was concerned, and somehow, he handled them all. Mostly because Red made him laugh and forget his sadness.

Just then, she spotted Marshall climbing out of his SUV, helping Olivia with her dog named Kat.

He moved with the easy walk of an athlete, one hand protectively on his daughter's shoulder. He wore a puffer vest that showcased broad shoulders and a strong posture, his head uncovered and giving her a good look at tightly cropped black curls.

Her gaze darted to the cream puffs again, the treats practically daring her to make a move.

Should she take them in with her? No, not with their kids both present.

They'd probably walk back to the parking lot together, like yesterday. When they did, she'd tell him she'd brought him something, hand him the box, and... suggest coffee.

Oh, boy. She'd rather crawl through broken glass, but wasn't that how her son felt about making friends? Someone had to break the ice and get uncomfortable.

Benny was already half out of his seat when she opened her door, Sir Isaac Newton bouncing beside him, nose pressed to the glass.

The second she opened his door, he spilled out with the pup, both of them a flurry of energy.

"C'mon, Mom!" he called, racing toward the entrance. "Sir Isaac Newton can be first if we beat her."

Gracie didn't want to beat them. She wanted to walk with them, but it was impossible as Benny shot off with his dog.

She waved to Marshall and Olivia as she hustled to keep pace.

Marshall called, "Hello!" in greeting, his smile visible from the distance, warm enough to give her the encouragement she needed.

She would definitely give him the cream puffs and her number. Today. Right now.

Tugging off her gloves, her hands sticky inside the leather, she followed Benny into the lobby. He zipped through sign-in, gave a quick wave, and marched off to the training room to be first.

"He's a doll," Renee said to Gracie as she replaced the clipboard. "So independent and smart."

"That he is," Gracie agreed, fighting the urge to glance over her shoulder and see if Marshall and Olivia had reached the door yet. She had to time this just right. "I was hoping he'd make some friends here."

Renee looked just dubious enough that Gracie knew Benny hadn't even tried. "His dog loves everyone," she said, clearly grasping at straws.

Gracie laughed, mostly because she was relieved that cool air blew in, which had to mean—

"Good morning, Olivia!" Renee called brightly.

Yes! Feeling a smile grow, Gracie turned, lifting her gaze in anticipation of seeing Marshall. But it was only Olivia.

"Where's your father?" Renee asked, echoing Gracie's thoughts.

"I just said goodbye to him." The little girl pointed over her shoulder. "He had to take a work call. I can sign myself in, Miss Renee."

Renee handed her the clipboard, but smiled at Gracie. "I'll encourage him," she said on a whisper. "Sometimes men just need a little push."

For a moment, she felt the blood rise to her cheeks. Was she that obvious? Then she realized Renee meant Benny, not Marshall.

"Thanks, Renee," she said softly.

"Oh, and Benny volunteered the actual Grumpy Santa to deliver our treats at the talent contest," she added, beaming. "That's a coup. Can we count on him?"

"Yes, you can. He's Benny's great-grandfather and he'll be here for sure."

As Gracie pulled her gloves back on, ready to walk out, she caught Olivia handing the clipboard back.

"Miss Renee?" the little girl said, so politely it hurt. "I want to use a dog whistle set to a certain frequency for my trick. Will that be okay?"

"Of course, honey," the woman said, gesturing toward the hallway. "You just practice it a few times and make sure the others know."

Oh, *no*. A dog whistle on a special frequency. Someone wasn't going to like that.

Sighing and hoping that didn't increase the rift between Benny and Olivia too much, Gracie stepped outside, just in time to see Marshall's truck approaching, catching him on the phone, laughing.

He stopped to let her pass, giving her a smile and friendly wave, intent on his conversation.

Well, she could hardly jump up and down and offer cream puffs and a coffee date now, could she?

Maybe next time. If there was a next time.

Chapter Seven
Nicole

By the second ski run, Nicole was utterly delighted to realize she was having fun. So. Much. Fun.

The conditions were great, the trails were groomed and, true to his word, her personal ski patrol had kept them on the easiest hills and greenest of trails.

"Homeward Bound," Cameron said, tapping the trail sign with the end of his pole as they slid off the top of Bald Mountain—Baldy, as any self-respecting local would call it. "That run is cruisy, pretty, and easy to feel like a hero."

He didn't need a lightweight run to look like a hero. He could have leaned against a fence post and it would have been swoony, but she liked that he wasn't trying to impress or intimidate her. He'd promised a low-key ski day, and so far he'd kept his word.

He was attentive, encouraging, and respectful, even gentle, in his way of handling the fact that she'd had an experience that had traumatized her.

After they pushed off, Nicole projected her focus outward, leaning into big turns and a gentle rhythm, just letting muscle memory return.

Hips to the fall line, hands forward, breathe.

Beside her, Cameron skated a few strokes and then, to her utter dismay and secret thrill, turned around and began to ski backward, facing her.

"You're doing great," he said, tugging down his mask so she could hear the warm steadiness in his voice. "See? I told you. Natural."

She snorted. "If I'm a natural, why do my calves feel like they're doing calculus?"

"Because they are," he said solemnly. "Skier math. Very advanced."

The mountain rolled out like a white ribbon. At every rise, Deer Valley unfurled another view of tree-clad hills, glades smoothed by wind, the curve of a ridge that broke and spilled toward town.

Cameron made a grand, exaggerated hockey stop that showered her with a dusting of snow. Then he executed a wobbly little spin that ended with him sprawled on the snow, limbs theatrically akimbo.

"Man down," Nicole announced, laughing.

"Tragic," he said into the snow. "Please send immediate assistance. Ideally in the form of a hug."

She skied past his outstretched pole and gave it a playful tap. "Denied."

He popped up with ridiculous ease, brushed off, and fell into pace beside her, forward this time. "Some first responder you'd make."

"Not much of one. Also, falling on purpose negates your assist."

Laughing together, they slid through a mellow S-turn where the run skirted the trees, which she steadfastly ignored. *Not today, old memories.*

"Looks like it might pick up later," he said, tipping his chin at the thickening cloud band building from the west.

"Could be a snow globe and an avalanche," she said.

"Yep." He squinted through his goggles. "Skies are capricious up here."

She smiled. "Big words for a ski bum."

"Don't make me race you, Nicky."

She cracked up at the name, and kept going to where the world fell away at an overlook. Below them, Park City sprawled like a postcard.

She caught glimpses of tiny buildings, a line of cars inching along, Main Street's lights blinking like a Christmas tree. It hit hard to realize how much she'd missed this extraordinary perspective of her world, the thrill of looking down from the top of a mountain.

They stood in quiet for a moment, poles planted, goggles up, puffing out breaths as they took it in.

"It's so beautiful," she said at last, which felt like saying a wave was wet. "It makes me feel...safe." She gave a quick laugh. "Which is the last thing I expected to feel up here."

He smiled down at her. "Then this was the biggest win."

Nodding, she held his gaze. "It's you," she said softly. "You make me feel that way."

He started to say something, a joke maybe, but closed

his mouth. "I'm glad," he said. "Means I'm doing my first responder job."

She had a feeling it was more than that, but didn't argue. Turning back, she looked out at contours of the resort. Tucked into the middle distance, off a shoulder of trees that guarded a little pocket of slope, she noticed a small wooden structure.

"What's that cabin down there?" she asked, pointing with her pole.

Cameron turned, peered, and smiled. "That, my friend, is the Powder Keg."

"What's that?"

"It's an ancient DV shack the resort used to use to stash extra tools and old signage, and for patrols to rest or ride out storms," he told her. "They moved to a more modern outpost, and the patrol has adopted it as a, uh, social center. I don't spend too much time there anymore, but the younger patrollers party there. When I go, it's to make sure no one's started a fire or broken a law."

"The Powder Keg? Cute name."

"Folklore has it that someone tapped a keg after a record snow dump in 2011 and the name stuck. It has a vibe, though."

"Can I see it?"

He glanced at her, a sparkle in his blue eyes. "Only if you follow the wipeout and whiteout rules."

"What are they?"

"First timers have to tell their biggest, baddest wipeout story."

"You already know mine," she said without hesitation. "And the whiteout rule?"

"You have to carve your name in the whiteout wall if you get snowed in."

She sucked in a breath. "Will we?"

He laughed and eyed the sky again. "If the snow picks up, we'll haul out. But..." He shifted his weight, considering the slopes. "Not gonna lie, getting there is a touch tougher than Homeward Bound. Not black diamond tough, but not as easy as we've skied all day. One short lift, then down a blue that gets steep in the middle. I'll be with you the whole way. Unless you'd rather not."

She didn't let herself think too hard. "Let's do it," she said, the wind catching the words. "I want to see this famous Powder Keg."

"More like infamous, but, yeah, let's go."

They slid off Homeward Bound where it widened and crossed a connector that fed into the lift maze for a short, steady chair. Next to each other on the lift, they shared a look through their goggles, their eyes crinkling in conspiratorial smiles.

As they rode, she felt a jitter or two, but let it pass. In a minute, they slid off the lift and headed right toward a drop-in marked as intermediate.

The first pitch looked steeper than she liked, but Cameron pulled up beside her and planted both poles.

"We'll do it in little bits," he said, his easy tone like a balm.

She took a breath and pointed her skis. "Let's go."

The first turn happened because she made it happen, not because panic twisted her legs in the right direction. The second came the same way, her whole body feeling like it was in charge.

By her third turn, she let the mountain do some of the work. When she checked to a stop by a towering pine tree that probably covered a deep well, she waited for low-key panic to kick in.

It didn't.

"Okay?" Cameron asked, matching her stop with ridiculous grace.

"*So* okay," she assured him.

The middle of the run was a little hairy, making her thighs sing with the effort, but then it all flattened as the cabin came into full view, nestled in a wind-carved notch like a secret place.

It was bigger than she'd expected, with a pitched roof and stone chimney, but made entirely from aged logs. Someone had hung about a thousand Christmas lights that she suspected never got taken down and tied gold ribbons around stairs up to the front door.

He popped his skis off and stuck them in the snow with a crunch. Nicole followed, grateful to release her bindings and march over the snow in boots.

Inside, the Powder Keg smelled like old wood and wet wool and maybe a little beer, which seemed appropriate for the name. A fieldstone fireplace filled one wall, with a stack of kindling and a note written in black Sharpie: *Don't be a jerk. Replace what you burn.*

A slouchy sofa of faded green sprawled through a

living room, sharing the space with some bean bag chairs. A mini-fridge hummed next to a sticker-covered Yeti cooler. An old percolator sat on a shelf with a jar of coffee, all under about seven avalanche beacons hanging in a festive row.

Someone had made a half-hearted attempt to decorate a small artificial Christmas tree with some cheap ornaments and clumps of old-school silver tinsel that hung like frozen tears.

"I know, I know," Cameron said with an apologetic shrug. "This place is half frat house, half cozy cabin, all... mountain."

"It's perfect," Nicole said, perching on a bench by the front door to take her boots off while Cameron toed out of his. "I mean, if you had to design a fort for brave kids, it would have looked like this."

He laughed at that, crossing the space to open a door to a back room. He glanced in, then closed it.

"Some brave, some just reckless, but"—he jogged up a set of stairs, slowing at the top to look through a wooden railing at a loft—"no one is here. I'm not surprised, since it's Christmas week."

As she poked around, Cameron found a lighter and coaxed a fire to life, and soon heat crawled into the room and into Nicole's bones. They slipped out of their jackets, tossed them on a bean bag, and settled on the green couch.

"Lots of chatter about a weather system on my radio," he said, picking up a small device clipped to his jacket, frowning at the screen. "But this looks bigger than the models said. If gusts hit forty, lifts'll shut down."

"But we can ski to the base from here, right?" she asked, glancing toward the window to see snow swirling harder.

"With me, you can," he assured her.

Relaxing a little, she turned to him. "So what's your best wipeout story?" she asked. "I know you're not a first-timer but I want to hear it."

His smile faded, giving her the impression it was a doozy.

"Break anything?" she asked when he didn't answer right away.

His mouth set and he looked right at the fire. "It's not...pretty. Or funny."

He sounded *so* serious. "I think that's the whole point of a wipeout story. Mine certainly wasn't pretty or funny."

His brows flicked. "Let's pick another topic."

She inched back, more from the tone than the request, but she nodded.

"Fine, but so you know, I'm not going to shy away from the tough topics," she warned him. "So, let's start with..." She gave him a playful poke in the arm, not surprised there were hard muscles under his ski sweater. "Relationships."

He chuckled. "You do like the difficult things."

"Hey, I just did a blue run for the first time in nineteen years. I feel powerful."

Smiling, he turned to her. "You start. Anything serious in your past?"

"Not really," she said without a moment's hesitation. "I had a long-term boyfriend all through high school, probably because he was the one guy at Canyon View High School who didn't ski. That was my prerequisite."

He rolled his eyes. "And look at you now. A date with a ski patrol."

So, it *was* a date, she thought, fighting a smile. "Right? All this time I've been missing the joys of the Powder Keg. In college, I dated one guy for a year, but we fizzled. And in the past five years, I've given my heart, soul, and time to building my business at the ski shed."

He nodded, considering all that.

"And you?" she pressed when he didn't offer anything.

"Me? You'd cry if you saw my schedule," he said on a laugh. "I drive forty minutes twice a week for classes at Weber State in Ogden, then I have, oh, I don't know, ten hours a week of ambulance ride-alongs—not working, but training. I do rotations in the ER, and patrol. Between all that and my, um, you know, family, I don't have much time."

"So you never date?" she asked, finding it hard to believe he didn't have plenty of girls—probably some who frequented this cabin—who would be happy to distract him from his busy schedule.

"Not really," he said. "I'm too serious about studying and working."

"Then why ask Bri for my number?"

A very slow smile pulled, and he tipped his head to her, a softness in his blue eyes touching her right to her soul.

"I'd love to say, you know, I'm a sucker for big brown eyes and all that pretty hair—which I am—but there was something about you..."

For what felt like five full heartbeats, he regarded her closely, as though he was trying to figure it out.

"My famous father?" she guessed, hoping so much that wasn't the attraction.

"No, absolutely not," he assured her. "I think it was your...vulnerability.'"

"On skis? You call it vulnerability. I call it scared out of my mind."

"No, it wasn't your fear. I didn't really see that, since people fall all the time, even experts. It was..." He breathed out a sigh. "I think I felt like I could trust you."

"With what?"

He swallowed. "My wipeout story and the...aftermath. You ready?"

She nodded. "When you are."

NICOLE GAVE HIM TIME, sensing that this was no ordinary ski tale. Checking the weather again, they decided they had time for some coffee, which he brewed. While he did, she asked him about the paramedic training.

"How much do you have left until you get certified?" she asked.

"One more year, then I'll take the National Registry Exam, which is grueling," he told her. "A written exam that I've heard MDs say they couldn't pass, then a hands-on station test."

"What's involved with that?" she asked.

He poured two mugs of coffee and opened a cabinet, producing powdered creamer and a bag of sugar that looked like it had survived more winters than her grandfather. He made a face.

"Black okay?"

"If I want to live," she joked, taking the cup and walking with him back to the sofa.

"The station tests are tough, too," he said, going back to the conversation. "I have to lead cardiac arrest management, pediatric emergencies, prove my airway skills, trauma assessment, the whole deal. Since I'm already a firefighter, I'll do that on the job, but it could take another six months to complete."

"Wow." She blew on her coffee, eyeing him over the rim. "That's impressive."

"Be impressed after I get licensed, but yeah." He took a sip of coffee and set the mug on the table. "It's been hard."

"Lifelong dream?" she guessed.

His expression darkened. "Well, it's part of the aftermath of my wipeout story, which I am now ready to share."

Silently, she put her cup down, too, and turned to him on the sofa.

"There were no skis involved," he said after a beat and a slow exhale. "But a lot of ice, swerving, and a cocky attitude from a kid who...should have known better."

She leaned closer, forgetting the snow, the cabin, the whole world. Cameron's voice had grown deeper and quieter, and she knew what he was about to share wasn't something he talked about a lot.

"I was sixteen and had a driver's license for a grand total of four weeks." He let out a dry laugh, but there was no humor in it. "We were driving back from Salt Lake— me, my mom and dad, and my little sister, Elise. We'd turned my sister's indoor arena lesson down in Draper into a Hale family outing that day. She competed in junior cross-rails with horses."

"Oh." Nicole felt her face brighten. "I loved to go see those shows," she said. "I always wanted to do that but just owned horses, never competed."

"Maybe you saw her. She was excellent, a natural before she was even ten years old. Really wanted to be a vet."

She stared at him, the past tense making her hold her breath. "And..."

"We were in our Subaru Outback," he said. "The quintessential Utah family car. The roads were wet, temperatures were dropping, and it was that time of day where the sun turns the whole mountain gold but blinds you at every turn. I was doing everything right, at least I thought I was. Under the speed limit, both hands on the wheel, Dad reminding me to 'ease up on the brake.'" He shook his head. "Didn't matter."

Nicole fought a groan of fear at where he was going with this story, picturing the two-lane road, the jagged ridgeline of the canyons, and a boy trying to prove he could handle it.

"A truck towing snowmobiles hit black ice and jackknifed right across the line. I tried to steer us away." He looked down at his hands, curling them like they still gripped the wheel. "Way too fast, too hard on the brake, like the rookie I was. We spun and the truck slammed into the driver's side back door, right where Elise was sitting. The whole panel crushed like crumpled paper."

Nicole let out a whimper at the image.

"The sound..." Cameron's voice cracked. "Metal on metal. Glass shattering. And Elise—screaming bloody stinking murder because her legs were pinned. Mom was crying, Dad was cussing, and I was just sitting there with the airbag in my face thinking, *what did I just do?*"

She put her hands over one of his, mostly because she could tell he was trembling and she desperately needed to comfort him.

"Dad broke his wrist and Mom still has a bad neck. I barely had a scratch. But Elise..."

She held her breath.

"Well, she rode her last horse that day," he whispered. "They saved her. I'll never forget the first responders and how they moved. Or the doctors or the surgeries or the months of trying to put her legs back together."

"Oh, Cameron." She squeezed his hand. "I'm sorry your family, your sister, had to go through that."

"She's a couple years younger than you," he said. "Just about to turn twenty-five. And she has permanent nerve damage, is paralyzed from the waist down, and gets around my parents' house in a wheelchair. Tough as nails, funny and bright and beautiful, but she will never have a normal life." He closed his eyes, guilt etched over his clenched jaw.

Nicole leaned back, taking in the story and trying to imagine how life could change in the blink of an eye.

"Everyone says it wasn't my fault," he added. "Legally, it wasn't. But I wonder if someone else behind the wheel—someone older—might've swerved just right, braked with more finesse. Maybe she'd still be whole."

Nicole's throat ached. "You were a kid, Cam."

"Yeah," he grunted. "But she's the one paying the price." He finally looked up, his eyes raw and unguarded. "That's why I do what I do. Firefighting, ski patrol, paramedic school. If I can save one person, maybe I'll balance the scales. And it's also why I never got...serious with a girl."

She frowned. "Why would that stop you?"

"Elise," he said, as if it should be obvious. "She can't really live alone, so she's my responsibility for the rest of my life. My parents are older. My mom was in her forties when Elise was born and she's facing seventy. My dad's five years older. They got married a little later in life, so..."

So he thought about their passing, and how he'd take care of his sister.

"Anyway, I have some, uh, baggage," he said, looking directly at her. "And I'll never, ever put it down."

The vehemence in his voice squeezed her heart, the sound of a man who genuinely loved his sister and had made a commitment to her. A man who wanted a potential girlfriend to know exactly what she was walking into. She respected that, and wasn't the least bit afraid.

"I'd like to meet her," she said. "If I could."

He blinked. "Of course you could," he said. "But I... you're...we..."

She smiled. "Why is this man stuttering?"

"Because you just make me like you more every minute," he admitted, laughing softly.

"Then my evil plan is working," she joked.

His smile faded as he searched her face and leaned closer. "I knew I could trust you," he said. "I don't know why, but I knew it when I met you. She's alone right now, but she insisted I come today because...I kind of talked you up."

She felt a rush of warmth to her cheeks, and covered with a laugh as she pushed up. "Come on, let's get down that mountain and go see Elise."

"Okay," he said, pushing up. "I love that—" He froze at the sight out the window, and sucked in a breath at the view that was nothing but white. "Yikes. We maybe talked too long."

Yikes was right. Could she ski in that?

He walked to the front door and cracked it, the wind

buffeting it into his shoulder and blowing in some snow as Nicole joined him.

When he finally got it open, they stood in the freezing cold, taking in the sight of a blizzard. The air was thick with flakes blown sideways. The line of trees that framed the porch had blurred to ghost shapes. The slopes they'd skied to get here were white-on-white and barely visible.

The lifts that ran near the cabin weren't moving, the chairs whipping in the wind.

"We're not leaving here tonight," he said softly.

"But your sister—"

"I can get someone to check on her. I'll call her now." He pulled out his phone. "Thank God, there's service."

"Maybe we could..."

"No," he said, tapping the phone. "I could, but I would never ask you to. No trauma on my watch."

"We have to stay here all night?"

He smiled. "No trauma with that either," he said. "Don't worry. There's some canned food, an air mattress that you can have, and plenty of firewood. We're snowed in, but safe. You know what that means?"

So many things she couldn't even begin to name them. "What?" she asked.

"You get to carve your name in the whiteout wall."

She had no idea what that was, but what mattered was letting her mom—and now her dad—know she was safe.

"Let me call my family," she said. "They'll be worried about me."

"I can talk to your parents if you like," he suggested. "Just to assure them you are completely safe. We'll stay warm, comfortable, and play board games all night."

She smiled at him, touched by the offer and by this tender-hearted young man who was not the carefree partying ski patrol she thought he was. He was nothing like she'd thought, and that just made her like him more.

"It's fine," she assured him. "But if there's Monopoly, be warned. I was trained by a master."

He laughed and just the sound of that made her feel safe and weirdly excited about being snowed in with him.

Chapter Eight
MJ

MJ stood in front of the open wardrobe looking at two outfit options she'd hung for consideration. The navy dress was the safe choice, of course. Crisp and simple and...businessy. The all-black silk sheath was... date night.

"Nope." She plucked them both from their hooks, rehung them, and pushed hangers to find her nicest black slacks. With those, she chose a cream satin blouse with a tidy black velvet collar, which said...holiday dinner with a friend.

She added delicate earrings that caught the light when she turned her head. Her hair—the only thing she was truly prideful about—decided to obey today, falling neatly to her shoulders, with her few silver threads barely noticeable.

If she was proud of her auburn tresses, it was because George used to run his fingers through her hair when they cuddled at night, and call her his "copper penny."

She swallowed, tamping down the thought of her late husband, who would probably tsk mightily at the idea of a dinner date with a guest. Well, he'd tsk a lot more mightily if he knew her sister said the other option was to do a Google search on a guest, which was beyond the pale.

"Not a date," she murmured, and slipped into low heels that could probably handle snowy pavement and certainly didn't look like they belonged in a kitchen. "Reconnaissance."

She smoothed the shiny blouse, drew a steadying breath, and left her suite with the simple goal—she'd ask questions without prying. That was all. She'd silence her sister's fears that something was amiss.

Cindy wanted to know why an unusually wealthy plumber had taken up a month-long residence at their lodge, shown interest in MJ, and gifted them with a stunningly expensive snowmobile for no apparent reason.

MJ understood her sister's misgivings—and Cindy didn't even know he had a different name engraved on his very expensive watch. Her sister did know they were having dinner tonight, and agreed that it was a great way to get those answers.

Matt was waiting just outside the kitchen in the oversized dining area where five tables were set and ready for tomorrow's breakfast.

He sat near a window, looking out at the snow tufted on the branches of the spruce outside. He wore a cable-knit sweater and dark trousers that weren't anything she'd ever seen on any plumber. Ever.

He stood when he saw her, his smile quick and unguarded.

"Mary Jane."

She smiled at the use of a full double name that no

man since the pastor who'd married her had used. "That's me."

"You look beautiful."

"Thank you, Matt," she said, not sure how to return the compliment. "Quite a storm out there today, wasn't it?"

"That was something. Your niece—Nicole?—is she all right now? You said she was stuck overnight?"

"She is. Poor kid doesn't go on the mountain to ski for twenty years and the first time, she's in a whiteout. She told my sister she's safe in a ski patrol lodge until they can get down in the morning."

"Good to know. The city roads are fine now, though. I checked the state plow maps and the weather cams before I booked. My rental is steady as a house."

His rental was a pricey Escalade, she knew, and it could handle whatever the Utah winter threw at it.

He crossed to her coat, lifting it from the back of the chair where she'd draped it, helping slip it on. The move was courteous and kind, and...date-like.

Outside, he offered an arm down a few steps to where his SUV, already running and warmed, waited. He opened the door for her, and she settled in, breathing through a mix of excitement and nerves.

"So," she said as he pulled out, "I'm curious. How did you ever find Snowberry Lodge? You came before 'Grumpy Santa' made us famous. Not that I'm prying," she added quickly. "Just hoping to get more long-term guests like you."

"A simple internet search," he told her. "I was

looking for something off the beaten path where I could spend a few weeks or so. Not a resort with a thousand identical rooms. I like family-run and the place appealed to me."

"Why Park City? Why Utah? Are you a Sundance Film fan? That's really what put us on the map."

"Nah, not a film fan." He gestured toward the winter-white world around them. "It's Christmas here. In Florida, it's sunshine and palm trees."

"Do you...always leave home at the holidays?" She tried to sound conversational and not like she was conducting an inquisition, but he slid an amused look that said she might have failed.

"I used to spend the holidays at my uncle's house in upstate New York and it gave me a hankering for snow at Christmas," he said. "This place certainly fit the bill. And after a few days here, I knew it was where I wanted to spend the month."

As they reached the outskirts of Park City, he asked more about Nicole's reason for not skiing as an easy change of subject.

She found herself telling him about the accident, and he asked lots of concerned questions, including if she got therapy.

"No, she didn't seem to want it at the time, and then she just claimed not to need..." She drew back as the car slowed at a valet. "Riverhorse?" Her voice rose. "This is very...nice."

He turned to her. "So are you, MJ."

Before she could answer, a young man opened her

door and welcomed her, easing her out of the SUV and under an overhang.

MJ's belly did a small, disloyal swoop. The last time she'd been at Park City's top restaurant, she'd been celebrating a wedding anniversary with George. Maybe their twenty-fifth? Twenty-sixth? She didn't remember, but it was a long time ago.

He'd admired the food, balked at the prices, and teased her all night for being too delighted by butter that was presented on a chilled plate. She'd been serving hers that way ever since.

Inside, the restaurant spread out in polished wood and white linen with art on the walls that celebrated the mountains, the West, and winter.

"We have a table by the window for you, Mr. Walker," the host said, and then they were shown to a cozy corner. There, candlelight glossed the rim of her water glass and the window framed Main Street, which was dressed for holiday perfection.

He barely glanced at the massive wine menu, leaning in to whisper, "Can't it just say red? I don't need something long and French."

She laughed. "I'll have the same."

They chatted about the ambiance, the menu selections, the view, anything but...each other. How could she ease into her interrogation, MJ wondered when the wine came.

The answer came in the sound of George's voice in her head...

Be honest, MJ. There is no other way.

George was so right. Honest was the only way.

"I have to know something," she started after an easy toast and their first sip.

"Anything," Matt said, brushing his moustache with two fingers.

"Why did you give us that snowmobile?"

He drew back as if he were expecting a different question.

"Well," he said after a minute of thought. "Because it made me feel good?" His voice rose as if it were a question he didn't expect her to understand.

"But it was expensive."

He waved off the comment, the move accidentally flashing the edge of the watch that cost enough to renovate one of their bathrooms...so, obviously, money didn't matter to him.

"You've, uh..." She swallowed and barreled on. "You've done quite well for yourself."

He gave a tight smile, his kind brown eyes suddenly fading with something that looked...guilty? Why?

"Nothing more than the right time, right place."

She doubted that. "As a plumber?" she pressed.

"I started with a van and a toolbox," he told her. "And I was good at fixing things and better at hiring people who were more talented than I was. Turns out, if enough water heaters and sinks in a hundred-mile radius break, a man can make a decent living."

Giving away snowmobiles and staying in expensive cabins for a month was more than "a decent living," but it was very clear he didn't want to talk about it.

Their server returned with a basket of bread that smelled faintly of rosemary and butter. Then they had an amuse-bouche consisting of a small spoon of silky topping with a micro-green perched like a hat. The first bite was a whisper of lemon and cream and a pop of unexpected salt that made MJ close her eyes.

"Good?" he asked.

"Indescribable. I wish I could cook like this."

"You're a great cook!" He practically choked the compliment.

She chortled at his sweet enthusiasm. "I'm a serviceable, untrained cook who can nourish people. This"—she beamed down at the precious dish—"is made by someone who studied in France with the goal of delighting tastebuds. Big difference."

"Did you want to study in France?" he asked, leaning in as if her answer was all he cared about in the whole world.

For the rest of dinner, they kept up an easy conversation, without a hint of interrogation, but plenty of questions. She told him about growing up in Snowberry Lodge, and he talked about his passion for fishing in his hometown of Destin, in the part of Florida known as the Panhandle.

That took him to telling her some stories, a little about the climate and culture of a state she'd never been to. He made it sound pretty, and she wanted to see this beach town that boasted of white sand and palm trees blowing in the sea breezes.

"It might as well be Mars to a woman born and raised in the Utah mountains," she said.

"And you don't ski?" he asked for the second time, surprised by the fact.

"I did when I was young," she said, trying not to drag the last bit of fish through the citrus beurre blanc that pretty much ruined all her sauces forever. "But George wasn't much of a skier. He liked to hike in the spring and, oh, I do enjoy that. The mountains in the warmer months are just incredible. The flowers, the smell."

"You talk about the spring a lot," he noted. "Which is surprising because I think of Park City as such a winter destination."

"Oh, it is. But spring is my favorite time of year," she said. "There's always this one day in late May when I step outside and the world takes my breath away. The peaks of the mountains have snow, but everything is turning green and coming to life. I want to spin around and do what my late husband called my 'full Julie Andrews' singing, 'The hills are alive!'" She didn't sing, but he threw his head back with a hearty, appreciative laugh.

"Tell me about George," he said, his voice low and interested. "He must have been wonderful."

She felt warmth in her cheeks, and not because she'd nursed a second glass of wine. Because he seemed like he cared, and that touched her deeply.

"He *was* wonderful. We were married almost thirty-eight years. We were so happy, but..." She heard her voice thinning despite her best efforts. "He had a stroke five years ago. At the dinner table, of all places. We thought—we thought we'd caught it in time. He went to the hospital, they did all the things, stabilized him, gave me hope. Overnight, he had another one, and—" She swallowed. It had been a long time since she'd tried to put the awful simplicity of it into a sentence. "He never woke up. He was fifty-seven."

"Oh, MJ. I'm so sorry." There was no pity in his face, just genuine, heartfelt sympathy.

"Thank you." She reached for her napkin for the tears she certainly hadn't expected to shed tonight. "I don't usually—" She gestured to the air. "Sorry."

"For loving your late husband?" He set his hand on the table between them, palm up, silently offering support. The simple gesture made her eyes sting again. "Never apologize for that."

She put her fingers on his in gratitude for the sympathy.

"And something tells me you haven't been out much in these past five years."

She just smiled. "Do I look like the 'go out on the town' type to you?"

"You look like the most trustworthy, nurturing, kindest, and sweetest lady I've ever met."

The compliment took her breath away, so overwhelming, she eased her hand away. "And what about you?"

He lifted his brows in question.

"Have you been married or..."

He nodded. "Twice, actually. Once, when I was

quite young, and it didn't last. No kids, no hard feelings, just a mistake. I waited a long time to try again, and did when I was just past forty. I married a woman named Diana who had three daughters and so many opinions, I didn't know where to go to be safe." He chuckled. "We stayed married for fifteen years, then about ten years ago, we split up. Again, not acrimonious, but now..." He looked uncomfortable for a moment, and MJ leaned closer, instinctively knowing this was the kind of insight and information she needed.

"But now?" she urged when he simply didn't finish.

"Now, I'm here, in Utah, at this spectacular restaurant with a charming lady. Would you like dessert?"

And...just like that, he changed the subject. *Why?*

"Gracie brought home some cream puffs," she said.

He lifted a brow. "Yes, please. Let's go."

And that, she knew, was the end of that moment of revelation.

For whatever reason, Matt Walker, who'd engraved his Rolex with the first name Graham, who paid in cash for everything—including this dinner, she noticed, as he slyly slipped a few hundred-dollar bills into the bill folder —was just not forthcoming about his past.

STEPPING into a kitchen lit only by the light under the stove and the Christmas trees outside the window, MJ slowed and felt her whole body tense. She heard it before she saw it—a slow, treacherous plink of water falling from the ceiling to the floor.

A leak.

"Oh, no," she murmured.

"What's wrong?" Matt asked, his ears probably not that trained to a problem at the lodge.

"Listen." She tapped the pendant lights over her work island, eyes up on the ceiling to search for the source of the sound.

"Eesh. I know that sound," he said. "It's...there." He pointed to the mudroom, a drip from the seam in the ceiling falling onto the tile floor.

She grunted in frustration, already moving for towels. "You must think this place is on the verge of extinction. Which wouldn't be wrong."

"What's above this?" he asked.

"Roof. And there's an ice dam somewhere."

"Not something we have in Florida," he said.

"The snow slides and then refreezes, and the water has to find a way out," she explained, stress squeezing at her. "We've patched and repatched and we cannot afford a new roof right now and—"

"Okay." He put a hand on her shoulder. "Breathe. Do you have a ladder? A snow rake? Anything like roof cement?"

"No cement, but the rest is in the stable," she said, turning one way, then the other. "I need more towels. I should change. I need—"

"You need to stay right here and let me go up there and handle it. Where in the stable?"

"You can't—"

He put a finger on her lips. "I can. In fact, that is my middle name. Is the stable locked?"

"No. The roof rake is bright orange and the ladder is the heavy one with the duct tape." She shook her head. "You don't have to do this."

"I know. But I want to. Let me figure it out and you make tea and dessert. We haven't finished our lovely date."

"It wasn't..."

A flash in his eyes told her that if she finished that sentence, she would hurt this incredibly kind man and she didn't want to. "It wasn't...enough," she agreed. "You're right. I'll make tea and you—"

"Will stop the leak. Gimme some time. Oh, I have an idea. Can you fill a sock with some calcium chloride?"

She drew back. Calcium chloride she knew—every homeowner in the mountains used it to melt ice. But... "A sock?"

He nodded. "A sock. The longest one you have."

After rummaging around a bit, she filled an old cotton ski sock with the pellets they used for the steps and knotted it, wondering what trick he knew for this.

A moment later, the mudroom door opened and Matt appeared, having changed into jeans, work boots, and a puffer jacket. Behind him, in the shadows, she saw the ladder leaning against the house and the roof rake on the ground.

"Sock?"

She reached out, the stuffed sock dangling from her hand. "Did you find the leak?"

"I found the ice lip that's causing it. If I can tuck this sock perpendicular to the gutter, it'll melt the path and stop the leak. For now, anyway."

"Wait, there, Florida man. How do you know this?"

"I told you—my uncle lived in upstate New York and I spent holidays with him in a really old house. This isn't an uncommon problem."

She nodded, accepting the explanation, then looking at the ladder. "Matt, it's slick up there."

"I've been on a few roofs," he told her.

"Not icy ones that are older than time."

He just smiled. "Trust me."

"I seem to be doing that an awful lot tonight," she breathed, but she followed him outside, the cold diving down the collar of her coat.

With the porch light splayed over the eaves, she could see it—the glistening lip of ice that had formed above the gutter, snow piled behind it with nowhere to go but into...whatever breach was up there.

He set the ladder and tested it, then tested it again. Then he climbed just high enough to lean the roof rake onto the snow, struggling a bit.

"Something is..." He stretched over the snow, his head disappearing from her view. "What the heck?"

MJ's heart dropped. "What is it?"

"Just a popped nail."

"Oh, is that all?"

He didn't answer, but banged at something, and then

began dragging careful loads of snow, creating a narrow trench along the eave.

"Sock," he called down, and she placed it in his free hand when he reached. He laid the sock across the ice and climbed a little higher, fearless, pressing it into place.

When he finished, he climbed down with easy grace, stepping way back and looking up at the roof with a critical eye, silent and thinking.

"Were you able to fix it?" she asked, wondering why he was so quiet.

"The leak, yes, but..." He screwed up his face and looked from one side of the roof to the other. "Maybe I'm imagining it, but does it look like that side is sagging a bit?"

She followed his gaze over the dining area and mudroom. "Maybe, but I think it's been that way forever. It's an old building."

"Yeah, and that's normal, but sometimes a popped nail means a support beam is cracked," he said. "I'm no roofer, but I'd get that checked ASAP."

She stifled a sigh. Yet another expense. "I will," she said. "And the leak?"

"If we're lucky, it'll chew itself a path and let the water out the gutter right there."

"What if we're not lucky?" she asked, hugging herself against the wind.

"Don't worry, Mary Jane. If there's one thing I am, it's lucky." He smiled at her, the porch light putting a gold rim on him. "Go inside. You're shivering."

She obeyed, both of them stepping over the towels on the floor.

"Let's give it an hour and then I can go back up to check on progress. I don't want to invite new disasters."

"There's always one right around the corner," she said, fighting absurd tears as she started the motions of making a nice cup of hot tea for both of them.

"Is it that bad?" he asked, perching on a bar stool to watch her.

"It's worse," she said, the adrenaline dumping after the spike caused by finding yet another repair. "The estimate for a new roof—which we haven't had since my mother paid for the last one—is..." She thought of the number. "Let's just say it might as well be a trillion dollars. We don't have it."

"Oh. I knew things were tight, but when something like this hits...it's demoralizing."

"The roof isn't even the first thing we need," she continued, her head buzzing. Maybe that wasn't adrenaline. Maybe that was the second glass of wine or the man who'd just swooped in like Mighty Mouse and saved the day.

Maybe she was tired of dancing around an interrogation—which she was terrible at—and just wanted a shoulder to cry on. And the shoulders on the man who was seated at her kitchen island right now were strong and sturdy and available.

"Cindy carries the weight of it," she said, turning from the kettle to look at him. "She's the numbers gal and she knows just how bad things are."

"I thought you were all celebrating the big win in December, with a full house."

"That paid the tax bill," she said. "But it'll be back next year and we simply cannot compete with the likes of the new Grand Hyatt, right on the lift line at Deer Valley, or the upscale, super modern, totally fabulous Airbnbs sucking the wind out of our reservations."

"How do you fix that?" he asked. "Marketing? Is that why you were asking how I found the place?"

She shook her head. "Obviously, we need to upgrade the lodge—repair the roof, renovate the kitchen and bathrooms in the cabins, put in new floors, wallpaper, lighting—it would take hundreds of thousands of dollars to do what we need. Six figures, and the first one isn't a one. Or a two."

"Would that solve all the issues?" he asked, genuinely interested.

"It would start, but..."

"But what?" he urged.

She gave an awkward laugh. "I'm sorry. This isn't your problem."

He leaned his elbows on the island, regarding her. "If money weren't an object and you could do anything with Snowberry Lodge, what would it be?"

He asked so seriously that she considered her response just as seriously. Not that it took too much thinking. MJ knew exactly what she wanted—she and Cindy had shared this dream since they were little girls.

"Well, if money grew on trees, then..." She got cups

and put them on the counter, looking in the fridge for the Sugarfall box, which was...empty. "It would make the cream puffs reappear." She turned and made a sad face. "Someone must have helped themselves to our dessert. It's okay, I invite the guests to..." Her voice cracked and before she took a breath, he was up and had his arms around her.

"I don't need a cream puff. I just need to hear your dream for this place."

"My impossible dream," she corrected.

"Pretend it's possible."

"Okay." She leaned into his strong and glorious hug, then closed her eyes and envisioned her fantasy. "We'd be a wedding venue."

"Really?"

She nodded, unable to fight the smile. "Yep, but it's so...out there that I don't even dare to dream it. Cindy stopped talking about it years ago, but I still think about our vision."

"Tell me."

She sighed, wanting to do just that. "In my imagination, we would knock out the whole suite where I'm living." She gestured toward the mudroom and her suite. "And we could add on a beautiful space with a cathedral ceiling and a wall of windows to capture the view. It would be specially designed for small, elegant weddings. Less than fifty people, and if I had a better kitchen, caterers could come in. We'd have year-round weddings because that space could open to the big back lawn, and maybe we could build a gazebo—"

"I love gazebos!" he exclaimed, his enthusiasm so sweet, she wanted to throw her arms around him again.

"So do I," she said, a little embarrassed by the tears that threatened, so she turned to the kettle just before it whistled. "I sound like Benny making his Christmas list."

"Nothing wrong with a dream."

She snorted softly. "A dream that's not happening, Matt. In fact, my sister wants to sell," she whispered, not surprised, since her body, brain, and mouth seemed to have a will of their own tonight.

"No!"

She blinked at the firmness of his reaction, looking up from the kettle as she poured steaming water into the mugs. "No?"

He shook his head, and something in his face changed—not hardening, exactly, but setting. "You can't sell Snowberry Lodge," he said simply. "You said it's in your DNA."

She quietly finished the pour and returned the kettle to the stove. "Sometimes," she said softly, "you have to do...what you have to do."

"But a place like this?" he countered. "Built by love and history and family? All the guests? All the memories and traditions and meals and your dreams for—"

"Stop," she rasped. "You're making it worse."

"I'm sorry." He lifted the mug of tea, letting the steam reach his face, then took a sip.

"Of course you're right," she said after a moment of staring at her own mug. "Selling is unthinkable. But it might be inevitable."

"Nothing is inevitable," he said, reaching across the island that separated them. "You have no idea what could happen. Look what Benny and Red did for this month."

"We can't count on those two forever," she said, trying to make it sound light, but nothing felt light right then.

It felt good, though, to share tea and sympathy with this man. So, so good.

"Listen," he said after a minute, cocking his head. "What don't you hear?"

"A leak," she confirmed, not really surprised that he'd fixed it.

"I should check the sock," he said after finishing most of his tea. "And then I should let you sleep. I'm pretty sure you'll be up at six making French toast."

"Five," she corrected. "And tomorrow is pecan pancakes."

He just smiled at her, the light in his eyes so warm and real it nearly melted her like that calcium chloride on the roof.

He reached for her hand, then caught himself, giving a tight smile. "Thank you, Mary Jane, for a lovely evening."

"No, Matt. Thank you for listening and being so..." She didn't even know where to begin and surely shouldn't gush. "Nice."

He gave a little salute goodbye and walked toward the mudroom, peering up at the ceiling, then looking over his shoulder to give her a thumbs-up.

Wordlessly, he scooped up the towels in one easy

move and put them on top of the washer. Then he walked out into the cold night and she could hear his footsteps on the ladder, the roof, then off to the garage.

MJ stood in the kitchen and listened to the hush settle back around her, letting the whole night press on her heart like a flower in a photo album—always there to be remembered.

She turned out lights one by one and walked to her little suite.

At her dresser, she took off the sparkly earrings and set them in the dish beside her watch. In the mirror, a woman looked back who had told a near-stranger...a lot.

She'd gone on a fact-finding mission, and now Matt Walker knew more about her than she knew about him. He knew her deepest dreams and secrets of her heart.

How on Earth had that happened?

She had no idea, but she'd had the best time and fell asleep with a smile on her lips.

Chapter Nine
Nicole

Nicole woke slowly, blinking against a pale stream of winter light that filtered through the mismatched curtains covering the Powder Keg's back bedroom window. For a moment, she didn't know where she was, and the unfamiliar scent of wood smoke and old pine only deepened her confusion.

Then it all came rushing back—the storm, the long night, and Cameron sitting across from her in front of the fireplace, their legs stretched toward the flickering flames.

Her heart warmed at the memory. They'd stayed up for hours, talking and laughing while the wind howled outside the old cabin until well past midnight. They hadn't played games, but stayed wrapped in blankets, her head on his shoulder while they talked about their childhoods, their passions, their lives, and loves...or lack of them.

On a sigh, Nicole rolled onto her side, hugging the thin blanket. The blow-up mattress he'd covered for her creaked beneath her as a smile lifted her lips.

Maybe it was the secret, special feeling of being trapped in a cabin in a storm, or maybe it was the undeniable chemistry between them. Maybe it was...real.

The thought made her heart jump a little, as it had last night when he finished getting this room ready for her and held her in the warmest embrace goodnight. He'd pressed his lips to her hair and said something sweet she didn't remember now, but only because she'd been wondering if she was going to kiss him.

They didn't kiss, but that didn't make their connection any less powerful. In fact, the build-up would just make the first kiss even better. And after last night, she was pretty sure there would be one.

She peeked toward the cracked bedroom door, hearing the low groan of the couch springs from the front room. He must be up.

She brushed her tangled hair out of her face and sat up, grateful for the privacy and the heater he'd found. He'd stretched out on the couch, saying he'd done it a hundred times after late-night ski patrol shifts. Still, she couldn't shake how gallant it had felt—him giving her the cozy spot, no questions asked, like it was the most natural thing in the world.

The clink of a metal scoop and the first aroma of coffee floated in.

"Morning, sleepyhead," he called from outside the door. "Did you survive your first official night at the Keg?"

Nicole grinned, her stomach fluttering. "Morning. Barely. Do I smell coffee?"

"Black and bitter."

"Be right there." After dressing in her under layer and ski pants, then using a small powder room, she padded out to find Cameron holding a mug and looking outside. He wore thermals and a long-sleeved black base layer that clung to his broad shoulders. His dark blond hair was damp, like he'd splashed water on his face.

"Come," he said, beckoning her closer. "Look at the world after a storm."

Outside, the storm's fury had been replaced by a crystalline stillness. Two feet of untouched powder blanketed the slopes, blinding white under the rising sun. The trees sparkled, weighed down by ice, and in the distance, the groomers were already making their slow, deliberate passes across the ski runs.

"It's like another planet," she breathed.

Cameron handed her a steaming mug, their fingers brushing briefly. "The calm after the chaos. Best part of a storm."

She sipped and nearly moaned. It was strong, and the warmth spread through her in the most heavenly way.

"Thanks for staying with me," she said softly, meeting his gaze over the rim of her mug as she sat at a rickety table in the corner. "You didn't have to, but you made last night...really nice. Cozy, even. Everything okay with your sister?"

"She claims to have loved the solitude." His smile turned sheepish as he joined her. "I liked being here with you. More than liked it."

Nicole's heart tripped over itself. She couldn't help the laugh that escaped. "Good, because I liked it, too."

For a moment, they just sat there, quietly sipping coffee while the golden morning light filled the cabin.

"You know," she said thoughtfully, "you're kind of a natural caretaker."

He arched a brow. "Caretaker? Sounds like a handyman for the garden."

"A protector," she explained. "Not just your chosen profession, but in everyday life."

"You think?"

"You made me feel safe last night, despite the fact that a major and probably very dangerous storm was raging."

"This place is solid."

"You're solid," she corrected, making him give in to a smile. "You just...take care of people without making a big deal about it."

Cameron ducked his head, clearly pleased. "Maybe more than people would like me to."

She frowned, not sure if she followed.

"I've been accused of smothering," he explained as he finished his coffee and stood. "But mostly by my sister. Oh, and don't forget you have one very important thing to do before you can officially leave the Powder Keg."

Nicole tilted her head. "I do?"

He nodded toward the far wall, where a massive wooden support beam stretched across the room. As she got closer, she realized the wood was covered with names—scratched, burned, and Sharpied into history.

"Oh, the whiteout wall," she realized, laughing as she bent to read a few. "'Shredzilla 2010'...'Powder Hounds Rule'...Wow, some of these are ancient."

"I told you, it's a rule," Cameron said proudly.

"Anyone who's ever been snowed in here has to sign the Whiteout Wall. It's like the Keg's history book."

Nicole ran her fingers over the rough wood, smiling at the quirky nicknames and doodles. A tiny snowman drawn in blue ink. A jagged heart with initials inside. Then she froze.

"No way," she whispered as a thousand goosebumps danced up her arms.

"What?" Cameron came over, peering over her shoulder.

She pointed to a neat, careful carving near the base of the beam.

Flying Jack Kessler 1982

"That's my dad!" she said, her voice a mix of disbelief and delight. "Oh, my gosh, he was, what? Seventeen? He must've been here with his friends."

Cameron laughed. "Makes sense. The locals all know about this place. And honestly, the Keg probably hasn't changed a whole lot since then."

Nicole traced the letters with a light touch, unexpectedly emotional. It felt like she was standing in her father's footsteps, like a bridge between the girl she'd been before her accident and the woman she was becoming now.

"He would love this," she murmured. "Skiing has always been our thing, even when I swore I hated it. Being here...it feels like I'm getting that piece of us back. Thank you."

Impulsively, she hugged him, and he held her tightly, neither of them caring about the bulky ski thermals.

When she pulled back, he handed her a Sharpie. "Your turn. Leave your mark."

Grinning through tears, Nicole carefully wrote *Nicole Kessler* and the year just below her father's name. And she snapped a picture with her phone because Dad would *love* this.

After that, they geared up, tugging on boots and zipping coats. As Cameron tightened his gloves, he glanced at her.

"So, what's your plan for the day?"

Nicole shrugged. "I texted Bri last night and asked if she'd cover the ski shed this morning, since I didn't know when we'd get back. I'll probably go to Snowberry Lodge and bore my dad with ski stories."

"Thrill him, more like."

She laughed, liking that he really understood that.

"Or...you could come back to my place and meet Elise."

Nicole froze. The invitation was so unexpected that she barely managed to keep her voice steady. "I—I'd love to. Really. But, um, can we stop by my townhouse first so I can change out of this?" She gestured to her ski gear with a sheepish laugh.

"Of course," he said warmly, clearly pleased she'd agreed. His grin turned teasing. "But only if you can keep up with me on the way down."

Nicole rolled her eyes. "Oh, it's on."

They stepped outside where the powder gleamed like sugar under the bright blue sky. The silence was almost holy, and Nicole's breath caught at the sight.

"This is every skier's dream," Cameron said reverently. "Two feet of fresh powder and no one else around."

They put on their skis and Nicole pushed off, bracing for fear. But the moment she sliced into the soft, forgiving snow, the whole world floated away and she went gliding through clouds.

Cameron whooped ahead of her, spinning in a graceful arc, and Nicole laughed, exhilarated. She followed him down the slope, her heart soaring. She'd follow him anywhere, she realized. Even to meet the sister he adored. Especially to meet her.

WHEN CAMERON TURNED his sturdy Toyota Tundra off the highway on the rural outskirts of Heber City, the whole world seemed to widen under an endless sky. The mountains around this valley were some of the most beautiful in Utah, rimming stretches of fields dotted with red barns, cattle, and spacious family ranches like the one he told her the Hale family owned on twenty acres.

"It's so pretty out here," Nicole said, forehead against the cool window glass as he shared stories about growing up in this bucolic area.

"It's different from Park City or even Salt Lake," Cameron said, glancing out the window as though seeing it through her eyes. "But I wouldn't live anywhere else."

She could see why he loved it. The Wasatch mountains glowed to the west, the sun winking through the snow-covered canyons under a deep blue sky. Outside of town there were no strip malls or hotels, just old brick houses, horses, sheds, and land.

They turned again onto a narrow lane flanked by cottonwoods, the branches glazed with ice. At the end sat a long, sixties-style brick ranch house that looked both loved and lived-in.

A wide carport hugged one end. Well beyond it, a much smaller second structure was tucked behind the tree line, bigger than a garage, but not a full-sized home.

"That's me," Cameron said, nodding toward the little house. "The permanent guest."

"Have you ever considered living a little closer to Deer Valley or Park City?"

"With three roommates?" He rolled his eyes. "No, thanks. Anyway, not only do I love this place, but I can keep an eye on Elise and on my folks. I know, by today's standards, they're not 'old' at sixty-eight, but I like to be nearby." He shrugged. "It works for me."

It worked because he put family over fun, freedom, or a fast-paced lifestyle that a lot of thirty-year-old men might want. She couldn't deny that she found that incredibly attractive.

He pulled into the driveway and killed the engine. A minivan sat under the carport, and Nicole instantly spotted the blue accessibility icon on the side door. A low ramp sloped up to the front door, with sturdy rails and non-slip treads dusted from the night's snow that blew into the carport.

"I know she won't go out today, but I have to salt the

ramp," he said, almost to himself. Then he glanced at Nicole. "You'll get used to ramps, low sinks, bars to get around. It's not out of a magazine, but this house is tricked out for Elise. She could live alone, which she likes to remind us regularly, but none of us would have that."

They sat in the quiet for a beat, not quite ready to end their long date with another person in the mix.

"Hey. About Elise," he said, breaking the silence. "She's a firecracker, just so you know. She talks about her accident easily, so you don't have to dance around the wheelchair. Figuratively. I suppose if you want to actually dance, she'd be all about it."

Nicole laughed. "I'm game if she is."

He didn't laugh, though. His face actually grew serious. "You should also know that I, um, have never brought anyone home for my family to meet."

Her heart did a slow somersault. "Really?"

"Really." He searched her face. "And I guess you won't meet my parents this time, since they're on a cruise, but Elise is, well, she's...really important to me."

"I get that."

"I wouldn't be doing this if I didn't *really* see something with you." He exhaled the admission, as though he'd been holding his breath to make it.

Her throat tightened. "I see it, too. I wouldn't be here if I didn't."

Then he smiled and it brought a light to his blue eyes. "Good."

With that, he hopped out of the truck and hustled

around to open her door before she'd completely finished taking off her seatbelt. Because...of course he did.

Inside, the house was warm and sunlit, a sweep of south-facing windows flooding the living room with winter brightness. The space was open—furniture arranged with clear, generous paths.

From the entry, she noticed a low, rolling coffee table in the living room with rounded corners, and space for a chair she imagined wheeled into place.

"Elise!" Cameron called. "Home!"

"I heard the truck." The clear voice came from the hallway. "I also saw the text that said 'bringing a friend,' so I got all beautiful."

She rolled out of the hallway with ease, propelling the chair with quick, practiced hands..

Nicole's first thought was that Elise Hale was bright, like sunshine and candlelight. Her golden hair was pulled into a loose half-knot with wispy, wavy strands framing a chiseled face. She had greenish-hazel eyes that had been carefully made up, a delicate pendant glinting at her throat.

She looked athletically strong through her shoulders and arms, with textbook posture. In fact, from the hips up she looked fully healthy, as though the chair was an extension of her rather than a limitation.

She grinned and leveled curious eyes on Nicole. "Oh, Camelot. You weren't kidding when you said gorgeous brunette. Hello, stunner."

Nicole laughed, warmth blooming. "Hi. I'm Nicole."

"Oh, I know who you are. I'm Elise," she said,

offering a hand, then laughing and opening her arms. "Please, who are we kidding? Girls hug."

Nicole leaned down and hugged her, and Elise squeezed back with surprising strength.

"Okay, you pass," Elise decreed. "You smell like pine and sunshine. Very on-brand, big bro."

Cameron rolled his eyes and kissed the top of her head. "Be nice, E."

"I am always nice," Elise said cheerfully. "Selective about it, but nice."

Nicole glanced around, taking in the four stockings hung on a mantle, each embroidered with a name—*Elise, Cameron, Nancy,* and *Jim.* There was a poinsettia on the piano, and a tree laden with mismatched family ornaments.

"Starving," Cameron announced. "Soup and grilled cheese work?"

"Yes," they said in unison, which made Elise wiggle her brows like this was proof of destiny.

While he headed into a kitchen just around the corner, Elise spun her chair and led Nicole into the living room.

"What I'm really starving for?" Elise said, gesturing toward the sofa. "Girl talk. Tell me all the things, Nicole. Where do you work? Why do you like my brother? And what is your skin care routine because, girl, you are glowing. Or would that have to do with question number two?"

Nicole laughed again, shocked at how this young woman could put someone at ease. It was a gift, really.

"Let me see. I run a ski rental and equipment sales business at Snowberry Lodge just outside of Park City. My mom's family has owned it forever."

She nodded. "Cool, cool."

"And I like your brother because he persuaded me to ski down a mountain again after nineteen years of steadfastly refusing because of an accident. And I wash my—"

"Hold up, Nicky." She raised her hand. "An accident? Are you my people?"

Nicole laughed again, but her smile faded. "I guess I am," she said. "But I didn't get hurt."

"Nicole almost died," Cameron corrected, calling from the kitchen where he was obviously listening to every word. "Fell in a tree well head first as a nine-year-old."

"Oh." Elise drew back, her long lashes wide to arched brows. "Impressive. I was ten, so, hey. We are practically sisters." She pressed her hands together. "But not like my brother. I'm surprised he didn't refuse to let you on the lift."

Nicole frowned, not following. "Why?"

Elise sighed and leaned in, whispering, "Maybe I'm the only one he suffocates." She shook her head and mouthed, "We'll talk later."

Nicole nodded, remembering Cameron's comment about the same thing. Instead, she got back on skin care, then the lodge, the ski shed, and, at Cameron's urging, a little bit about her famous father.

But it was Dad's return to run the sleigh rides that brought a soft gasp from Elise.

"You have sleigh rides at this lodge?" she asked.

"Oh, yes. They—"

"Then you have horses." The longing in her voice was palpable.

"One," Nicole said. "Copper, who is sweet and gentle and sometimes stubborn and occasionally ridiculous. Addicted to peppermints and..." She stopped talking, stunned by the tears that pooled in Elise's eyes. "Cameron said you love horses."

"More than life itself," she said simply. "I love everything about them. And I miss them."

Nicole nodded, a sharp pang of empathy in her heart. "I felt that way about skiing," she said softly. "I didn't know it until yesterday when Cameron took me out again and we..." She searched the pretty face across from her, seeing the yearning in those beautifully made-up eyes. "Could you ever..."

Elise glanced down at her lap, then up again, expression frank. "I *could*," she said. "But I can't."

"What do you mean?"

"I could get on a horse and ride it—not like I did before, obviously, but people in my condition do it at therapeutic riding places all the time."

"Why don't you? What do you mean you 'can't' if you...can?"

She made a face. And poked her finger repeatedly in the direction of the kitchen. "My self-appointed knight in ski patrol armor won't let me," she said, very soft, so he definitely couldn't hear over the sound of sizzling from the stove.

Nicole leaned back on the sofa, considering this new twist.

"Maybe you could ride mine," she said before she let herself think too much about it. Surely Cameron wouldn't refuse his utterly adorable sister the chance to sit on a gentle horse and slowly walk the paddock? Could he refuse her anything?

Elise stared at her, quiet for the first time since Nicole arrived.

"I'm sure it's complicated," Nicole said, thinking out loud. "But we have this contraption at the lodge—my grandpa built a ramp and we had a harness for a guest who came every year. Whistler, our old horse, used to take her around our fenced-in paddock and the lady was just so happy. It took a little strength to get her on the horse, but she rode."

Elise's face lit brighter than the lights on the tree behind her. "Therapeutic riding places have the lifts and platforms. I know exactly what you mean. If I could just—"

"No," Cameron said, appearing in the living room doorway with a spatula in one hand. His tone wasn't harsh, just immediate, protective instinct firing. "It's not safe."

"Cam—" Nicole started.

"I'm not trying to be a jerk," he said gently, looking between them. "It's the falling that scares me. If she falls wrong...no. We can't take that chance."

Elise looked skyward, the classic eyeroll of a younger sister. "Oh, please. He thinks if I ride once, I'll ask to go every weekend. He's not wrong." She lifted a shoulder. "I miss it so much, it's stupid."

"Falling would be stupid," Cameron said. "It's not worth the risk."

But the look on Elise's face said *anything* was worth the risk.

"I understand," Nicole said slowly, considering each word. "I respect the caution. But this wouldn't be me slinging her up bareback to dart over hill and snowy dale. We'd be in the paddock. Slow. Safe. I mean, I know I saw that ramp and harness when I pulled out the sleigh last month."

He looked torn, then sighed and retreated to the stove. "Soup's ready," he said, not quite conceding.

While they ate in the sunny kitchen, Elise kept up the chatter, entertaining them and luring Nicole into conversation over delicious grilled cheese sandwiches.

After lunch, Cameron wiped his hands. "I'm going to jump over to my place, shower, and throw on something that doesn't smell like snow and cheese. You two okay without a babysitter?"

"We'll try not to set anything on fire," Elise said solemnly, then winked at Nicole. "Come sit. Tell me all the things you can't say in front of Cameron the Killer of Joy."

When the front door clicked, Elise pivoted her chair to face Nicole head-on, mischief replaced by something earnest.

"This is big," she announced.

"You riding a horse?"

"Oh, that? A dream I dare not dream," she said, flipping her hand with exaggerated faux drama. "No. I mean him and you. Cameron doesn't date, you know. He's absolutely certain no one could fall in love with him because he has me, the twenty-four-year-old millstone around his neck who will never be gone."

Well, she was blunt. And wrong.

"You're so not a millstone," Nicole said. "You're... amazing. And he loves you very much."

Elise's eyes filled, maybe a bit of an easy crier. "I know. He saved me in a thousand ways after the wreck. But I don't want to be the reason he misses his life. I want him to...have a wonderful life with a good woman and his own family." She bit her lip and blinked. "If you're part of that, then I am already your biggest fan."

Nicole laughed and touched under her own eye. "You're going to make me cry."

They looked at each other for a moment, quietly connected.

Nicole sighed and leaned closer. "What about riding?"

"I'm in. I mean, if there's a ramp, a harness, and a sainted creature with four legs who will tolerate me, then yes, I would like to sit on a horse again. Once. Twice. Whatever we can manage without making Mr. Safety's hair fall out."

"We can try," Nicole said. "I'll do what I can on my end."

"Might take some magic, Nicky."

Cameron came back after what felt like no time at all,

freshly showered with damp hair that was just unfairly attractive.

"You two good?" Cameron asked, amused and wary of the power of two bonded women.

"Perfect," Elise said. "Go take your girlfriend home and do whatever she tells you to do."

He choked. "Girlfriend?"

"She's gorgeous, sweet, and laughs at my jokes." Elise shrugged. "I demand you keep her."

Nicole hugged her new friend goodbye, the embrace even warmer on the way out.

"I got this, girl," Nicole whispered into her hair, getting a grateful squeeze in response.

Outside, the air bit their cheeks and the snow squeaked under their boots. They climbed into the truck and closed the doors, the cab going instantly quiet.

Cameron put his hands on the wheel, but didn't start the engine. "I know what you're going to ask," he ground out.

Nicole slid her hand across the console until her fingers found the back of his. "Let her ride my horse in the paddock, Cameron," she said softly. "She needs that. I promise you she'll be safe. My horse is sweet. My paddock is small. We'll lock her into the saddle and stay with her every step. Cameron, that girl *needs* to ride."

He closed his eyes with a long sigh. "I knew this would happen."

"That she'd find out I had a horse and want to ride it?"

He opened his eyes and turned to her, leaning in

closer. "That I'd fall so stinking hard for you, I can't say no to anything."

She felt her lips lift in a smile, but before she could take her next breath, he covered those lips with his, kissing her with just enough pressure to make her toes curl.

"Is that a yes?" she whispered.

He threw her a look. "Stop it. Stop being perfect right this minute or I'll...I'll..."

"Kiss me again?" she asked hopefully.

"Yeah. That'll happen."

She settled into her seat, unable to stop smiling.

Chapter Ten
Gracie

Red took charge of their small mid-week family dinner, and Gracie couldn't be more grateful for her grandfather's skilled touch when it came to comfort food. Tonight, he'd made a cast-iron pot of chili, taken some down to the lodge, and kept a portion for the three of them to enjoy.

Gracie sat at the round kitchen table, her head still at Sugarfall, with New Year's Eve just a few days away. They were almost done eating, and Benny and Red were deep in conversation about the upcoming dog talent show, chatting about whistles and tricks and what treats and toys Santa should bring.

"I don't know, Grandpa," Benny mused, sliding a spoon around his chili. "I like the idea of Santa, but it's New Year's Eve. Maybe we should think bigger."

Red's eyes flashed. "Things never go good when you suggest that, Benny-bean."

"But Santa's so anticlimactic."

"Anti..." Red snorted. "You were paying attention when we did that crossword puzzle, weren't you?"

Benny just grinned. "Am I right? We need Santa to do something more exciting. Got any ideas, Mom?"

"Something fun from the bakery?" she suggested. "We could bring New Year's Eve popcorn balls for the kids."

"Popcorn's awesome, but only fun if we make it," Benny said, then sat up as an idea occurred.

"We have a popcorn machine out in the back of the garage," Red said, chuckling as though just thinking about that thing made him laugh.

"Oh, no you don't," Gracie said. "It's a hundred years old and won't work without propane and…prayer."

"The Cornucopia? Not quite a hundred years old, but it works," her father said defensively, turning to Benny. "My father, your great-great-grandfather, Owen Starling, built that machine for the first Summit County Fair out in Coalville when I was younger than you."

"Really?" Benny's eyes grew wide. He was always fascinated by the family history.

"Yes, sir. He used an old wheelbarrow as the base, put a brass kettle under glass, added a copper spout, and if you put a bowl just so"—he held out an imaginary container—"it'll catch the corn as it pops."

"Cool!" Benny exclaimed.

"Daddy called it Starling's Superior Snacks. He ran a booth at that fair every August until Cora and I took over years later." He looked off into the distance, lost in a memory. "I loved that contraption."

"Let's bring it to the contest!" Benny said, bouncing with excitement. "We could make popcorn for everyone and I bet I can figure out a way to tie it into Newton's laws."

"Or just fake it," Red said on a laugh. "Who's gonna know but you?"

He rolled his eyes. "Olivia."

"Whoa, hold up there, boys," Gracie said, stopping this popcorn train before it got any further down the tracks. "We can't—"

She looked down at the table when her phone buzzed. She'd left one of her top bakers at Sugarfall to work on two cakes, so she flipped the phone, hoping there wasn't a problem at the shop.

At the sight of Sam Sutton's name on the screen, her heart dropped.

Of course he was calling to cancel. Of course he'd made a promise he wouldn't keep. Of course Benny would be disappointed.

"Sorry," she muttered, standing up to take the call and get the bad news without Benny having to hear. "I have to…talk for a second." She added a cautionary finger, ready to steer them away from the popcorn machine, but she was probably about to crush Benny in another way. So she tempered her warning. "Be sure you two know what you're doing with that thing."

Benny and Red exchanged a secret smile, which was never good.

But neither was a call from Benny's father about to deliver a dose of disappointment.

"I won't be long but do not let Grandpa clean up," she said, giving Benny's shoulder a squeeze when she walked by. "He's worked enough today."

"I promise, Mom," he said. "And then we'll get started on that whistle, okay, Grandpa?"

"I might be practicing that 'objects at rest stay at rest' law with Newt," Red cracked.

"Grandpa—"

"I know, I know. That's not his name. Kiddo, I don't have enough time left on Earth to call that dog by a fifteen-syllable handle."

As Gracie walked out, she pressed the phone to her chest, hoping Benny would still be laughing when she told him that his father wasn't coming to the doggie talent contest.

Grabbing her jacket from the hook, she stepped out the back door. It was cold, but Benny was famous for carrying on one conversation while eavesdropping on another, so it was better to talk outside.

The air slapped her cheeks as she stepped onto the back deck, pulling the coat tighter around her. She drew a steadying breath and swiped to answer.

"Hello?"

"Hey, Grace." Sam's voice came through warm, almost friendly, which immediately put her on edge. He never sounded like this unless he wanted something.

"Hi," she said cautiously. "Everything okay?"

"Yeah, yeah. Everything's fine. How's your day been? How's the bakery? Benny doing okay?"

"The bakery's busy," she said, wary of the unexpected small talk. "And Benny's great. Loving dog camp." She cut to the chase to shorten the call. "What do you need, Sam?"

There was a beat of silence, then a heavy sigh. "I didn't want to say this in front of Benny in the car the other day," he began, his voice lower. "But, uh, Coco and I are separating. We're getting a divorce."

The words landed like a punch. "You're...what?"

"It's not working out," he said roughly. "We've been fighting nonstop. It's...bad, Grace. Really bad."

She didn't even know what to say. Questions tumbled through her mind like an avalanche. Why now? What happened? Who decided this? What about their child? Would Sam just go through life leaving single mothers in his wake?

But she forced the thoughts back, keeping her voice even. "I'm sorry to hear that. Truly."

He gave a humorless laugh. "Yeah. Me, too."

Gracie bit her lip. Sam had always been complicated —charming and infuriating, equal parts brilliance and selfishness. Once upon a time, she'd been hopelessly, head-over-heels in love with him. She'd believed every promise.

Then she got pregnant and...*pfft*. The promises shattered and their love evaporated. She thought they might go have a quick Las Vegas wedding. He went to Las Vegas, all right.

Alone. And he stayed there.

She'd been heartbroken, but she'd survived. Her family rallied around her, and then helped her raise Benny. Her son had become her reason, her anchor, her joy in the darkest times, like when her father died.

But Sam? He just drifted in and out like an unpredictable, disruptive winter storm, leaving messes in his path.

"Grace," Sam said, breaking into her spiraling thoughts. "I didn't call just to dump my drama on you."

"Then why *did* you call?" she asked, sharper than intended.

"I..." He hesitated, and she heard the faint sound of a hand dragging over stubble, a sigh.

Here it comes. *I can't make it this—*

"I miss you guys. Can't wait to see you this weekend."

Her heart stuttered. *Miss you guys.* Not just Benny—*you guys.*

"You miss..." She couldn't even form the sentence.

"You and Benny," he clarified quickly. "I miss...what we had. I don't know. Maybe it's stupid to even say it."

Maybe?

He was divorcing another woman. What was wrong with him?

Gracie's mouth went dry. Shock rippled through her, tangled with anger and confusion. For years, Sam had kept her at arm's length, showing up only when it was convenient, never once hinting that he regretted leaving. And, now...this?

"I—" She swallowed, shaking her head. "Sam, I don't even know how to respond to that."

"You don't have to," he said gently. "I just needed to tell you."

The silence stretched, then she drew in a shaky breath. "I need to go."

"Yeah," Sam said quietly. "Of course. Grace, listen,

there's more I want to say, but it can wait. I'll see you on Saturday. What time is the big show?"

She looked out at the dark night, scowling. She should tell him not to come. Not to bring his problems and promises and lies.

"I'll text you the info," she said instead. "Bye, Sam."

"Bye, Grace."

She stood in the cold, staring at the snowy yard without seeing it. Her mind replayed his words on a loop. *I miss you guys.*

It shouldn't matter. She knew Sam was an unreliable, selfish man who had shattered her trust and her heart. There was no future there—not for her, not for Benny.

And yet...

Benny. Her chest ached. She'd been worrying about him constantly these past few months. He had no father, lost his grandfather when he was in kindergarten, and needed someone to guide him through boyhood into manhood. Red did his best, and Jack had stepped in with kindness and steady strength, but it wasn't the same. A boy deserved his dad.

She thought of Benny's face lighting up when Sam actually showed up for something, the golden, rare moments when Sam's attention was fully on him.

Gracie wrapped her arms around herself, shivering despite the coat. She couldn't—wouldn't—let herself hope that Sam wanted to be that kind of father to Benny. Even if he *did*, she could never trust him again.

Still, his words clung like the cold. *I miss you guys.*

When she finally went back inside, she plastered on a

smile for Benny's sake. He was loading the dishwasher and still talking about cognition in dogs, while Red sat at the table, looking wiped out and satisfied.

As she passed, she gave her grandfather's bald head a kiss. "Great chili, Benedict Starling."

He smiled up at her, then back at Benny. "Gracie, I love that boy," he said under his breath. "Don't know what I'd do without him."

She felt tears sting at the words. Did Benny really need his father when his great-grandfather was right here, being all the man Benny needed to emulate in life?

MUCH LATER THAT NIGHT, Gracie paused outside Benny's door, easing it open just enough to peek inside.

The room was dark except for the soft glow of his spaceship nightlight, which cast pale blue beams across the ceiling where stick-on stars glimmered faintly. Benny lay sprawled sideways in his bed, the covers a tangled mess around his legs. His mouth was slightly open, his breaths deep and even.

Beside the bed, Sir Isaac Newton snoozed in his crate, his little chest rising and falling in time with Benny's breathing. Good boys, both of them.

This was her world, she thought. This child, this dog, even. This simple, ordinary moment. She slipped quietly inside and tugged the covers up over Benny's shoulders, pressing a kiss to his warm forehead.

"I love you, sweet little man," she whispered, though he couldn't hear her.

She lingered a bit longer, letting the sight of him sink deep into her bones. But even that tender scene couldn't fully push away the rattled feeling left behind by Sam's phone call. His words echoed in her head.

Gracie bent over to peek at Newt, who opened one eye to acknowledge her, but didn't move.

She blew him a kiss and slipped out, easing the door closed behind her.

The living room was dimly lit by a single lamp. As she padded past on her way to the kitchen, hoping for a bite of something sweet and maybe a cup of herbal tea, she spied Red sunk into his old recliner, as expected.

Years ago, Mom and Dad would be in there with him, reading or playing a game. But her mother had essentially moved into the lodge since Dad died, and Gracie understood why. It had been five years, but George McBride had been a presence in this house, and a good one.

Red sat with a pair of reading glasses perched low on his nose, tapping a pencil on a clipboard where he'd printed out *The New York Times* crossword puzzle. He claimed finishing it daily kept him sharp.

He glanced up over the rims of his glasses, his bushy brows rising. "You look like the bad guys won."

She gave a faint smile. "Just the battle, not the war."

He pointed his pencil toward the empty chair beside him. "Come over here, granddaughter. Let's have a chat. And by chat, I mean what's a six-letter word that ends in

C and is..." He scowled at the fine print. "'Like the Mona Lisa?'"

She thought about it. "Six letters that ends in C? That's all you have?"

"There's an O in the third box."

"So not...classic?"

"That's seven."

"Mythic?"

"Has an O, assuming Benny was right and a 'modern way to make an exit without leaving' is 'ghosting.'"

She gave a soft chuckle. "Where does that boy get his brains?"

"Forget brains, he's got heart," Red said. "Just like his mama. And by the way, the popcorn maker really does work."

She narrowed her eyes at him. "You wouldn't."

"I might."

Rolling her eyes, she pointed to the kitchen. "I need tea and something sweet. How about you?"

"Only if you come back and talk to me," he said. "Something's on your mind."

She gave him a knowing smile. Red Starling was truly amazing. He never pushed, but when he invited a talk, she knew she'd come away wiser and better for it.

"Okay," she said softly, heading toward the kitchen. "Let me brew us a cup."

She returned with two steaming mugs and a small plate of biscotti she'd brought home from the bakery, trying to decide if she should tell him about Sam's call.

Part of her wanted to shove the whole thing into a

box and lock it tight. But Red was a sounding board and she needed one.

She handed him a mug and sat down, curling one leg beneath her. Red sniffed the tea, nodded in approval, then took a sip and studied her closely. His eyes, old but still sharp, didn't miss a thing.

"Mm-hmm," he moaned as it went down hot. "So save us both the suspense and tell me what's weighing on you."

She broke a piece off her biscotti, chewed slowly, buying herself a few seconds. Finally, she sighed. "I was going to tell you eventually anyway, so...Sam is coming to town. He wants to see the dog talent contest."

Red's lip curled like he'd just bitten into something sour. "Benny mentioned that, but I'll believe it when I see it."

She nodded. "Exactly. I honestly thought he'd cancel at the last minute, like always. Benny would be crushed, and we'd have to pick up the pieces."

"He *will* cancel," Red said darkly. "That man's made a career out of disappointing that boy."

Gracie winced. "I thought so, too. But this time... might be different."

Red looked sharply at her. "How so?"

"That was who called at dinner. He and Coco are getting a divorce."

Red snorted. "Big, fat shockeroo." His voice dripped with sarcasm. "He can't get along with anyone. Always looking for the next shiny thing, and when that loses its luster, he bolts. Quitter. Leaver. Loser."

Despite her heavy heart, Gracie managed a dry laugh. "How do you really feel?"

"I feel like our lives are better off without him. You?"

"I don't know what to think," she admitted. "We talked, and it was...strange. He told me he and Coco are fighting, that it's really bad. And then he said..." She hesitated, the words catching in her throat. "He said he misses us. Benny and me."

Red's head jerked up, eyes flashing. "If that no-good fool comes sniffing around trying to sweet-talk you, you tell him to take a hike in the mountains and get lost."

"I'm not going to—"

"I mean it." His voice was rough with emotion. "He broke your heart. More than that, he lets that boy down time and again. A man, if you can call him one, doesn't change. He's lonely, blue, and feeling like he's made yet another mistake."

He was so right.

Gracie wrapped her hands around her mug, soaking in the warmth. "I've built a life without him." Her voice softened. "But it's been ten years, you know. Same year Aunt Cindy and Uncle Jack divorced. And now they're—"

"A totally different situation," Red insisted.

"But Benny does need a father figure."

Red's expression softened, though his eyes stayed fierce. "He's got me."

"He does," Gracie said quickly. "And you're the best. But you're his great-grandfather, not his dad. It's...different." She swallowed hard. "I know I should probably try dating, try to find someone, but it's scary. Weird. Hard. When I meet someone, I kind of freeze up. I'm not bubbly or outgoing."

Red leaned over and put a hand on hers. "You're a prize. You're a Starling! You've got Cora's strawberry blond hair, MJ's big beautiful heart, George McBride's brains, and my...backbone."

She blinked fast, fighting tears. "What if that's the answer I've been looking for all along? What if Benny could finally have his dad in his life the way he deserves?"

"Sam?" Red's jaw tightened. "You don't need a man who only shows up when it suits him. That boy needs stability, not empty promises."

Gracie let out a shaky sigh as she sank deeper into the chair and sipped her tea.

"I just don't know, Red. I share a child with Sam. Part of my heart will always...belong to him, I guess. Not in a romantic way, but because of Benny. Because we're all connected by DNA."

Red shook his head. "Don't confuse history with hope, Gracie girl. That man had his chance, and he blew it. Don't let him blow up your life all over again."

She nodded, even as doubt prickled at the edges of her thoughts. "You're right," she whispered. "You're always right."

But as she nibbled the last bite of her biscotti, she couldn't quite silence the treacherous voice inside her head.

What if this really was the answer? What if, against all odds, Sam meant what he said? What if Benny could have his father back, and she could stop worrying about filling that void herself?

Red reached over and patted her knee, his eyes soft now. "Want to know what I think?"

"Always."

"Sam won't show. And the popcorn popper would make Benny happy."

"It would," she reluctantly agreed.

"Can I bring it?"

She sighed. "You would even if I said no. That thing is iconic."

He stared at her for a minute, then sucked in a noisy breath. "That's it! Iconic! Six letters that ends in a C. Thank you!"

Sipping her tea, she just smiled at him, feeling a wave of affection for her precious grandfather. "No, Red, thank you. And, yeah, bring the Cornucopia. That'll be awesome."

And maybe, she thought with a smile, it would give her an excuse to talk to Marshall Hampton.

Chapter Eleven
MJ

The kitchen had gone quiet at last. MJ wiped her hands on a dishtowel and let out a long breath after a busy day.

Cindy and Jack had gone to town for a late dinner together, so MJ had eaten Red's chili alone, which was a welcome break. She dealt with a few guest issues, and now, at well past ten, there was peace. And...loneliness.

She waved the towel as if she could use it to swipe away that silly thought. MJ wasn't lonely. She worked non-stop, had her daughter, grandson, father, sister, and niece within hugging distance most of the time, and her "alone" time was rare.

But it was in those rare windows that she missed George the most.

Tucking the dishtowel over the handle on her oven, she turned and looked at the mudroom ceiling, still dry after Matt had fixed it.

The temporary patch held, but the sight of it filled her with a strange, gnawing frustration that was probably the real source of her discontent. Things falling apart meant...money. And money meant...worry. And worry meant...selling the lodge. And selling meant...

MJ's life was...over.

"Oh, stop it," she murmured to herself, rooting deep for the positive attitude that had carried her through every moment in life—her childhood, her marriage, becoming a grandmother, losing her mother. Even kissing her husband goodbye in a hospital room with a promise to come back in the morning...only to learn he'd died overnight.

Through it all, she believed the cup was half-full, even if it tipped over and spilled sometimes. If they had to sell Snowberry Lodge, she'd still have her family, and, really, what else mattered?

Home, a voice in her head whispered. That's what mattered. With a sigh, she turned to survey her little kingdom, the kitchen of Snowberry Lodge.

The brass fittings were tarnished, the paint peeling behind the sink. As she crossed to the pantry to return a bag of cocoa powder, MJ's sharp eye picked out more chips, discoloration, and a slightly crooked cabinet.

Everything was small enough to ignore in isolation, but somehow painted a picture of a world—a *life*—fraying at the seams.

She stopped in the middle of the room, fighting tears. If this is just the kitchen, she thought, what about the guest rooms? The cabins? The bathrooms?

Cheap repairs. Quick fixes. Band-Aids on problems that needed surgery. The truth was, they were barely keeping up appearances, and they were in a very precarious position.

It wasn't just the lodge getting old, outdated, and sad. It was...MJ herself.

Walking to the window, she looked at her reflection in the dark glass, not liking what she saw at all. She turned, refusing to go down some sad hole of...of sadness. George always said, "Wallowing won't fix a thing."

And right now, a lot of things needed to be fixed.

Just as she stepped into the hall, the front door banged open, letting in a rush of cold mountain air and a chime of laughter.

Cindy and Jack swept inside, cheeks flushed from the cold and a special happiness that MJ hadn't seen on her sister's face in a decade. They were arm in arm, heads bent close, laughing softly like teenagers, unaware of her watching them.

MJ smiled despite herself. Gracie had a phrase for this—*the love bubble.* And these two were smack in the middle of one.

Cindy looked ten years younger these days, her wheat-toned hair loose around her shoulders, her eyes sparkling. Jack's hand rested possessively at her waist, his grin boyish and unguarded. Watching them like this— rekindled, renewed—lifted her heart.

MJ didn't need to have that kind of love but, goodness, she was so dang happy that Cindy did.

"Well, don't you two look like trouble," MJ teased, folding her arms as they came toward her. "I was beginning to think you'd run off and eloped."

Jack chuckled. "Not yet. We just got caught up talking after dinner."

"It's the most beautiful night in town," Cindy said, practically cooing the words. "You know, that lull between Christmas and New Year's Day, and everyone is relaxed and happy. Main Street is still shimmering and all the snow globes are lit. It's gorgeous." She looked up at Jack, who gave her a squeeze.

"So are you," he said, staring at Cindy like he had the day he'd watched her come down the aisle.

MJ's heart gave a bittersweet twist. She was genuinely joyous for her sister, but the sight stirred something deeper—a whisper of hope she tried to smother.

Maybe life didn't end at their age. Maybe love wasn't a closed door after all. Her mind flickered to Matt and the way his deep laugh warmed her. She pushed the thought away before it could take root.

"Hot chocolate?" MJ offered, lifting her chin toward the kitchen. "I was about to have a cup."

"Only if there are marshmallows," Jack said, rubbing his hands together.

MJ shot a playful look. "What kind of lodge do you think I'm running? Marshmallows and, if you'll stoke it, a blazing fire."

As she headed back into the kitchen, she heard Cindy whisper, "Something's wrong. She's got that look."

Of course her sister could see right through her false brightness.

But she didn't want to drag this happy couple into her blues. As she finished making the cocoa, she gave herself a little pep talk, ready to keep the conversation light and merry with two of her favorite people on Earth.

But when she walked back into the living room, Cindy's concern was written all over her face. "Spill it," she said, accepting the mug. "What's going on?"

She'd never get anything past her sister, the closest thing she had to a soulmate since George died.

MJ sighed and sank into her favorite armchair near the fire that Jack had brought back to life. The flames painted the room gold, flickering over the worn furniture and family photos.

Yes, she could share some of her concerns. It would be strange if she didn't.

"It's just...that leak Matt fixed," she began. "It's holding for now, but it made me notice other things and realize..."

"We're in bad shape," Cindy said on a sad sigh. "I know."

"I don't want to dwell on it, Cin," she said. "Not now, with you two"—she lifted her mug—"so good again."

They shared a quick smile, but their expressions grew serious.

"We're good, not blind," Cindy said. "We got through the worst of it and are paying the tax bill, but you know what I've said for more than a month. We do have"—she glanced at Jack—"another option."

Did he think they should sell, too? MJ turned to him, holding her breath. Because if he did—

"It's crazy to even talk about," he said, swallowing a sip. "You can't give up Snowberry Lodge."

MJ huffed out a relieved breath. "Thank you. But we

are looking at some major problems that are starting to eat away at me."

Cindy narrowed her eyes. "Worrying is not like you, MJ. I expect you to see blue skies, not stormy ones."

"I know." MJ rubbed her forehead. "But I can't help it. Everywhere I turn, I see something that needs attention, and it's like...like I'm standing on a frozen lake, and I can hear the cracks forming under my feet."

Jack frowned. "Hey, now. Cindy's right. This isn't like you at all."

MJ wrapped her hands around her mug, seeking warmth. "The thing is, I keep imagining what we *could* do. We could restore the place while keeping its soul intact. Fresh paint, new fixtures, better insulation. A new bathroom in every cabin, and, of course, the dang roof." She didn't dare mention her wedding venue fantasy, not when they had to be down to earth and practical about this. "Any chance you called the roofer? Matt didn't like what he saw up there."

She nodded. "He'll be here January second. I'm just praying he says we can go another year or two without a new roof."

"Or a For Sale sign," MJ said glumly.

Jack leaned forward, elbows on his knees. "Look, you two. There are ways we can get through this. I can help with repairs."

"It's not just patching holes and painting walls," MJ said. "Some of these problems are big—hidden stuff like plumbing, electrical. Expensive things."

"This place is worth a fortune," he said. "You could always get an equity loan."

Cindy and MJ shared a look, this topic well-discussed by them.

"We hate that idea," Cindy said, speaking for both of them.

"We don't want to saddle Nicole and Gracie with debt," MJ said. "If something should happen to us..."

"Nothing will happen," Jack said confidently, "but I understand the position."

"And if we did sell?" Cindy looked from one to the other. "Those girls would be set for life."

Jack nodded. "I get that, but I'm sure they'd rather have Snowberry for another generation than a fat bank account."

"I know Nicole would," Cindy said. "But Gracie has a child."

"Gracie would weep if we lost this place," MJ said. "But she'd also weep if she owed the bank two hundred thousand dollars and couldn't pay it back."

The conversation trailed into silence. The only sound was the crackle of the fire and the faint creak of the old lodge settling for the night.

MJ swallowed the lump in her throat. "I just...I want to believe that we can keep this place going forever. But what if we can't?"

"We'll figure it out together," Cindy said, pushing up. "I need to head home."

MJ rose to gather the cups. "All right, you two. I'm going to put these in the sink and crash."

"I'll walk you to your car," Jack said to Cindy, "then hit the hay myself. More sleigh rides tomorrow, and I'm as tired as Copper."

She gave them both a warm hug and carried the cups into the kitchen. She was still thinking about the conversation when she heard a tap on the mudroom door.

This late?

She walked over, kind of hating that she hoped it was Matt. And really hating the dip of disappointment when she opened the door and found Jack.

"Oh, hi. Is everything okay?" she asked.

"So okay," he said, grinning like a fool. "Never been better, MJ."

She laughed lightly, ignoring the cold air to just take in the contentment on his face. "Another cocoa?"

"No, but I need a favor," he said.

"Anything, Jack."

"Can you organize a New Year's Eve party here at the lodge? Nothing huge, just the family and close friends. I'd like...to have everyone together."

She frowned but nodded. "We usually have a gathering on New Year's Eve. Something special?"

"I'll say." He slid into a slow smile, his dark eyes shining. "I'm going to ask Cindy to remarry me."

She gasped and took a step backward. "Really?"

"I want to ask her right at midnight and start the New Year with her as my fiancée," he announced, as proud as any young man who planned a proposal.

"Jack," MJ said with a sigh. "That's so sweet."

"And I want the whole family to know how much I love her."

She pressed a hand to her lips, tears welling. "Of course I'll arrange it."

"Thanks, MJ." He gave her another hug, tight and long. "You're the best sister. And you're freezing."

She inched away from the open door. "But my heart is warm. I'm happy for you."

"Thanks. G'night."

"Goodnight, Jack." She closed the door and stood unmoving in the mudroom as his footsteps faded.

Cindy was getting married. Well, remarried. To the only man she'd ever loved.

She leaned against the door, the wood cold through her sweater, trying to understand how she felt.

Overjoyed, of course, for the sister she loved with every cell in her body. Worried, because they had no real solution for their problems. And lonely, which was the one that troubled her the most.

Was she envious of Cindy? No, not MJ. She didn't have a jealous bone in her body.

She simply felt like she was holding on to everything by a thread...and she was afraid it was going to break. How would she get through this kind of uncertainty?

She had no idea, except that, right now, that loneliness hit harder than ever before.

Chapter Twelve

Nicole

The stable smelled of fresh hay and leather mixed with the earthy tang from Copper's stall. Chilly December air snuck in through the wide sliding doors, so Nicole tugged her gloves tighter.

She stood beside her father, watching him test the buckles on a sturdy leather saddle they'd pulled from storage that morning. Beside it, neatly stacked on a wooden bench, sat the rest of the specialized gear they'd need—an adaptive mounting ramp, a body support harness, and a side-walker belt Nicole had borrowed from a therapeutic riding center a few towns over.

Nothing was going to happen to sweet Elise today—except a dreamy ride with Copper.

As if he knew he was part of something special, the big guy snorted and whinnied, his ears flicking in anticipation.

"Does it all look okay to you, Dad?" she asked, crouching to check the ramp one more time. The wood was solid, sanded smooth, with a gradual incline wide enough to accommodate Elise's wheelchair.

"Okay?"

They turned at the sight of Red meandering into the

stable with a grin on his face. "I built that beauty for a lady who came here with her husband every spring for a decade or so."

"I remember her," Jack said, straightening. "They came from Minnesota, as I recall."

Red nodded. "That lady, Gayle was her name, loved Whistler, but lived in a chair. Her husband told me about this ramp and harness they had made and I fashioned one for her visit the next year."

"That was sweet of you," Nicole said, coming closer to her grandfather. "Was it easy to get her up and down?"

"I did it with her husband's help, and yours, Jack."

Her father nodded. "We got her saddled and back down again without a single problem."

"Whistler was a little bit more mellow," Red noted, walking over to give Copper's head a stroke. "But I think you're up for the task, big fella."

Nicole smiled, gratitude spreading through her chest. "I know. I just want it to be perfect for Elise. She's so excited."

Jack reached out, brushing a stray piece of hay from her shoulder. "I'm proud of you, sweetheart."

"Thanks, Dad. That means everything."

"So this Cameron guy..." His tone shifted, teasing but laced with protective undertones. "You must really like him."

Nicole laughed, half groan, half giggle. "You don't waste any time, do you?"

"He's your father," Red said. "If he didn't ask, I'd worry. And then *I'd* ask."

She leaned against the ramp, exhaling slowly, looking from one man to the other.

"I like him a lot. It's crazy how fast it's all happened, but it feels...like it could get real." She looked down, tracing a line in the sawdust with her boot. "He's kind, Dad. The way he takes care of Elise blows me away. He's not just a protective big brother—though he definitely is that," she added with a laugh. "He's nurturing, like he actually gets joy from making her life better."

Jack's brow furrowed thoughtfully. "And when he's not doing that he's a firefighter in the off-season, and ski patrol in winter."

"And taking paramedic training."

"Careful that halo doesn't slip," Red cracked, making them laugh.

"He sounds like a good man," her father said.

"He is." She met her dad's eyes, her heart swelling. "I really want you to get to know him better today. More than that quick handshake on the bunny slope."

"Looking forward to it," Jack said sincerely.

As if on cue, the low rumble of an engine approached. Nicole and Jack moved toward the wide barn doors just as the handicap-accessible van pulled up on the drive to the stable.

After he parked, Cameron hopped out, bundled in a dark parka, his breath puffing in the cold air.

"Morning!" he called, giving Nicole a smile that definitely took away the cold.

She jogged toward him, excited that he'd agreed to do this. "Morning! Perfect day for a ride."

Jack followed, extending his hand. "Good to see you again, Cameron."

"Mr. Kessler," Cameron said, shaking firmly. "Thanks for letting us do this."

"Call me Jack. And it's our pleasure."

While they exchanged greetings, Nicole rounded to the passenger side as the van's hydraulic lift whirred. Elise appeared, radiant and glowing, her hair braided beneath a knit beanie. Her grin was wide and uncontainable.

"You ready for this?" Nicole asked.

"I haven't slept all night," Elise admitted with a laugh, practically vibrating with excitement. "Let me at that horse!"

Nicole hugged her tightly, the metal of the wheelchair frame pressing against her coat. "You're going to love Copper."

As Cameron maneuvered the chair down the ramp, his movements careful and precise, Nicole caught the flash of tension in his jaw. He was excited for Elise, but his concern radiated like heat.

Jack seemed to notice, too. "Don't worry," he said in his calm, steady way. "We've done this before. Safety's our top priority."

Cameron nodded, though his knuckles were white on the handles. "I know. It's just..." His gaze softened as he looked at Elise. "She's my little sister."

"And your biggest pain in the butt," Elise teased, rolling her eyes. "Relax, Cam. I'm not made of glass."

"Let's meet Copper," Nicole said, her voice bubbling

with excitement as she took over the wheelchair. She guided Elise into the stable, where Red was standing in front of the horse, the ramp, and the rig.

"This is my grandfather, Red Starling," Nicole said. "And my baby, Copper. This is Elise, our rider."

Elise gasped, her hands flying to her mouth as she met Copper's big gaze. "Oh. My. Gosh. Nicole, he's...he's beautiful."

"I get that a lot," Red joked.

Elise pointed at him, not missing a beat. "I can see why."

Red chuckled and stroked Copper's big head. "Copper's a fine boy. Smarter than some folks I know." His weathered face creased into a grin.

Cameron came in with Jack, and Nicole introduced him to Red, all of them talking and laughing about the big day.

Cameron crouched beside Elise's wheelchair, his voice soft. "You ready, E?"

"Ready doesn't begin to cover it," Elise said, her hazel eyes bright with excitement. "How are we going to do this?"

Jack joined them, looking serious. "Okay, here's the plan. We'll roll Elise up the ramp until she's level with the saddle. Then, using the transfer sling and side-walker belt, we'll help her pivot and swing her leg over. I'll stabilize her upper body while I secure the harness. Cameron, you can support her torso until she's fully seated."

Cameron's throat bobbed as he swallowed. "Got it."

Red gave a little snort. "I'm just here as the ramp

engineer and chief architect. If it breaks and you go south, it's on me."

"You made this?" Elise asked. "That's incredible."

"We'll see how incredible it is when you're on it," he replied.

"Are you seriously concerned?" Cameron asked, worry in his eyes. "Because if you think—"

Red cocked his head and gave him a look. "Do you really think I'd let her get on it if I thought it was less than one hundred percent chair-worthy?"

Cameron lifted a shoulder. "Of course not. I trust you."

"She's a waif compared to the lady I built it for," he said. "Plus, she's so excited, I think she could fly up to that saddle. Let her roll, boy."

Elise beamed at him. "I like you, Red!"

"Back atcha, kiddo."

"All right," Jack said. "Let's do this."

Working as a seamless team, they positioned the wheelchair at the base of the ramp. Elise's hands gripped the armrests, determination shining in her eyes.

"Here we go," Jack said, wheeling her carefully up the incline. Copper stood steady, calm and patient.

At the top, Nicole clipped the transfer sling beneath Elise's hips, adjusting the straps for perfect balance. Cameron crouched beside her, murmuring reassurances.

"You're doing great, E," he said.

"I know," Elise said, her voice trembling with emotion. "And this one ends with me on a horse. A handsome, amazing horse." She patted Copper's mane, and he stayed perfectly still, rising to the occasion.

On three, they lifted gently, pivoting Elise so Nicole could lift her right leg over Copper's back. She was light as a feather, but the absolute deadness of the weight in her hand stunned Nicole.

She knew Elise was paralyzed from the hips down, but until she actually guided one of those non-functioning legs into position, the reality of that hadn't really hit her.

This girl had half a working body, and more spirit than a lot of completely whole people. She could be a bit much, a big personality, even, but that just made Nicole love her more.

As Jack buckled the adaptive saddle straps and secured the safety harness snugly around her waist and thighs, Elise reached down and brushed a hair off Nicole's face.

"Thank you," she mouthed.

They shared a long, connected look and Nicole impulsively blew a kiss. "Have fun."

Cameron's hands lingered protectively on Elise's sides. "Are you sure it's tight enough? Double check the buckles."

"It's secure," Jack assured him, giving each strap a firm tug.

"Boy," Red said, shaking his head, "you'd bubble wrap her if you could."

"Probably," Cameron admitted with a self-deprecating snort.

Elise rolled her eyes affectionately. "Cam, I'm not falling off. Chill."

Finally, Nicole took Copper's lead rope while Jack positioned himself at Elise's other side. Cameron hovered close, clearly battling the urge to hover even more.

"Easy walk, boy," Nicole murmured to Copper, clicking softly.

The horse stepped forward, slow and steady. Elise's breath caught, then broke into a wild, joyful laugh.

"Oh, my gosh, this feels so good!"

Nicole's vision blurred with tears as she and her father guided Copper out to the paddock and strolled on his favorite circuit, while Cameron and Red leaned against the rail, watching.

Nicole stole a glance at them, her attention fixed on Cameron's attractive features. But it wasn't his good looks that had her heart right now. It was the sheer love in his eyes as he watched his sister fulfill her dream. Protective worry, yes, but unabashed joy, too.

Elise lifted her chin, exhilarated. "I feel amazing, Nic," she whispered. "Like...like nothing's impossible."

"Sometimes, nothing is," she replied.

Copper's hooves crunched softly on the packed earth and, for a few perfect minutes, the world felt whole and shiny.

When Elise finally asked to stop, Nicole slowed Copper and steadied him back in the stable while Cameron and Jack helped her dismount. Once back in her chair, Elise grabbed Nicole's hands, eyes glowing.

"Thank you," she whispered, voice breaking. "This was the best day of my life."

Nicole knelt beside her, hugging her fiercely. "You can come ride Copper anytime you want. Consider him yours, too, Elise."

Looking up, Nicole met Cameron's gaze, his whole expression filled with gratitude and something that made her nearly tumble right down to the hay-covered stable floor.

Elise beamed through her tears. "Next time, maybe we trot."

Cameron groaned. "She has to push the envelope," he murmured.

Nicole laughed, hugging Elise again as Copper nuzzled her shoulder, the perfect punctuation to a perfect morning.

A LITTLE WHILE LATER, the air was still humming with the magic of what they'd done. Elise smiled the whole time Nicole tended Copper and the men took the equipment down.

Jack clapped Cameron's back. "Hey, before you go, could you give me a hand putting all this gear away?"

"Of course," Cameron said immediately.

"Appreciate it," Jack said. "And I hear you're a firefighter. You handy with broken things?"

Cameron threw a look over his shoulder, catching

Nicole's eye with a question in his. "Uh, yeah. What do you need?"

"A hinge outside. Come on. I could use the muscles."

"I'll come, too," Red said. "Even though I'm apparently just a pretty face." He winked at Elise. "Good job, equestrian."

She smiled at him as he walked out.

"Your grandfather is certifiably wonderful," she announced as Nicole threw some fresh feed in Copper's stall. "And you get your striking dark looks from Daddy, huh?"

Nicole laughed, wiping her hands on her jeans as she came back to the wheelchair. "Well, Mom's blond, so probably. Come and meet her. You want to go in the lodge and get warm?"

"No. I want to sit in this stable and smell horse for... well, ever."

"Aww." She looked around the stable, seeing it through Elise's eyes. "I get that."

"But I do want to meet your mom and aunt, and see the inside of this gorgeous lodge." Elise started to push the wheels.

"I got you," Nicole said, rushing to the back to grab the chair handles.

"No, please." She looked up over her shoulder. "I'm quite capable of getting around by myself, despite what Cameron would have you think."

Chatting happily, they went side by side over the path that her father had so thoughtfully cleared. Nicole took her to the mudroom door, since there were no steps, and helped her in over the threshold.

As soon as she was in the kitchen, Elise inhaled deeply, sighing. "Okay, the stable smelled good, in a horsey kind of way, but this?"

"This is MJ McBride's kitchen," Nicole announced. "Heaven on Earth."

Elise looked around, her eyes wide as she took in the country kitchen, the pine table in the bay windows, and MJ's gleaming workspace.

Nicole's mother appeared, peeking into the kitchen. "I thought I heard voices."

"Mom!" Nicole said, hurrying to her side. "This is Elise—Cameron's sister. Elise, this is Cindy Kessler, my awesome mom."

Cindy's expression softened with a warm smile. "Oh, honey, I've heard so much about you. It's so nice to finally meet you."

Elise reached up a hand. "Nicole's told me all about you, too. Thank you for letting me crash your beautiful lodge."

"You are welcome anytime," Cindy said, shaking her hand and adding a light hug. "How was the ride?"

"Life-changing," she quipped, looking up at Nicole. "I love your daughter."

Mom laughed. "That makes two of us."

"Three, if you count my smitten brother."

Nicole flicked at Elise's fingers. "Oh, hush, you."

Mom lifted a brow. "I just met him outside," she said. "Handsome and kind, and apparently had a toolbox in his truck that impressed Jack. So, thumbs-up."

"He's a good guy," Elise said. "A little overprotective, but good."

MJ swooped in from the dining area. "Oh! Company! This must be the horsewoman everyone is talking about!"

Elise laughed at the gushing, easily chatting with them as MJ made warm drinks and set out snacks.

Nicole guided Elise into the living room and parked her chair near the sofa. She sat cross-legged on a chair beside her, feeling suddenly grateful for her own easy mobility. Elise handled the transition like a pro, and never complained.

"You have the best attitude," Nicole said, sensing she didn't have to edit her thoughts. "I mean, I know it can't be easy, but you're just...so positive."

Elise shrugged, the color in her cheeks deepening at the compliment. "Well, I figure I can either be bitter about the chair or just...live my life, you know? Doesn't mean I don't get frustrated, but I don't want to waste time being angry. I'd rather master skills and grow myself."

Nicole's heart ached with admiration. "That's incredible perspective. Honestly, I think you're one of the strongest people I've ever met."

Elise laughed softly. "Oh, you barely know me."

"I know enough," Nicole insisted, certain her assessment was right.

Once they were settled with some cookies, Cindy and MJ drifted back to their respective tasks, leaving Nicole and Elise alone to wait for Cameron to join them.

Elise took a sip of tea, then sighed dramatically. "I'm not kidding when I say today was the best day I can remember in years. Thank you, Nicole. Really."

"You're obviously a natural with horses."

"All animals, if I'm being honest. I adore all living things equally."

"I'm surprised you don't have a dog," Nicole said.

Elise made a face. "I did, but Freddie died a year ago and I haven't had the nerve to fall in love again. Anyway, I..."

Nicole looked over at her, waiting for the rest.

But Elise just shook her head. "Cameron's just too protective. He's like a third parent—on steroids."

Nicole frowned, not sure she saw the connection between that and not having a dog.

"I mean, I get it, I do," Elise continued. "But I'm capable, Nicole. I can get around, assuming there are no stairs. I'm smart, I'm independent, and I'm twenty-four years old. I want a life. But my family—especially my brother—treats me like I'm so fragile."

Nicole reached over, squeezing her hand. "You are capable. I can see that, and I'm sure Cameron can, too."

She gave a dubious look. "He's a tad hardheaded," she said. "Camelot thinks he knows what's best for me. And the burden of all that blame wears him down."

"He was at the wheel," Nicole said. "Of course he's going to blame himself."

"Well, I don't blame him," Elise said. "So that should be enough for him to let go."

Nicole nodded, knowing these were tough landmines for a brother and sister to navigate.

Elise closed her eyes. "Can I continue our candor and be totally honest?"

"Of course."

"At the risk of sounding like a cliché, I..." She glanced at the door as though she expected Cameron to walk in any minute. "I have a dream," she finished.

"What is it?"

"I want to be a veterinarian."

"Cameron mentioned that when he first told me about you," Nicole said. "And you'd be an astounding vet."

"Small animals, yes, I think—I know I could be. Paraplegic people have careers, you know. There are some limitations, but it isn't impossible. Anything *is* possible, like you said."

"Have you looked into it?" Nicole asked.

She snorted. "Oh, I went way past looking. Dragged myself through the online applications, and have done three video interviews. But..."

Nicole sat up straighter with each statement. "Elise, really? You've—"

She held up a hand. "I've done the whole thing in secret, Nic. My parents—especially my dad—are not fans of the idea and Cameron won't even talk about it."

"Where? What's the program? Is it online or what?"

"It's in Eagle Mountain, which is west of Utah Lake, a good hour and fifteen minutes from our house," she said.

"The school is called the Great Basin Veterinary Institute, which was created with the Department of Agriculture and a coalition of ranchers and wildlife organizations. It's an accredited vet school that embraces the traditional and non-traditional student. Which I certainly am—plus, I am not their first handicapped or wheelchair-bound student."

Nicole pressed her hands together, loving this. "This sounds perfect."

"So perfect. They take thirty students a year. Thirty and they *want* me. I have one interview left."

Nicole's jaw dropped. "This is extraordinary! When are you going to tell Cameron?"

"We talked about it, but he doesn't know I've applied and interviewed." She swallowed and blinked hard. "Look, I'm an adult and I can make my own decisions. Of course, he's vehemently opposed, but only because he can't drive me an hour and fifteen minutes each way. For one thing, he goes an hour in the opposite direction for paramedic school and his schedule is crazy."

"Maybe someone else can take you."

"I don't want anyone to take me," she said. "I want to live on campus, which is where all the vet students live. It's a very immersive program and you can get a degree in three years, plus an internship."

Nicole leaned back, considering that. "You should do it."

"Of course I should. Get this—the dean has to make his final decisions this week on next year's class. He said he'd be in his office on Saturday morning—New Year's

Eve! He has invited me for the final interview at ten A.M."

Nicole searched her face. "Well?"

She lifted a shoulder. "For one thing, Cameron's scheduled to work that day from eight to three. And he'd never—"

"I'll take you!" Nicole shot forward.

Elise put her hand over her mouth as if she couldn't believe yet another dream was coming true for her. Then her face fell. "No. No, he'll never forgive you."

"What? He can't be that opposed to—"

"Opposed? He'd blow a gasket if you drove the van or took me somewhere."

Nicole frowned. "For your dreams? To be one of thirty chosen for such a prestigious program? Could you really live there?"

"Yes! They have student housing and I discussed handicapped access with one of the administrators on my second interview. They have two first-floor apartments that are wheelchair accessible with some minor assistance from other students. I'd be fine! I'm young and strong and..." Elise's voice cracked. "No one wants to give me a chance to prove that. And by no one..."

"You mean Cameron," Nicole whispered.

For a moment, they just looked at each other and Nicole's head whirred with thoughts. If she took Elise, it could cost her this new relationship with Cameron. But if she didn't, it would haunt her forever. And Cameron had to see—

They heard laughter and men's voices in the kitchen.

"I'm taking you," Nicole announced under her breath.

"Without telling him?" Elise challenged.

Nicole swallowed. "He'll be at work. We'll go, do the interview, and be back by early afternoon. I can still make Benny's dog show, and then you *have* to tell him the truth. Promise? As soon as he gets home."

"What if he's mad at you?"

She lifted her shoulder. "Then he's mad. I'm going to do what I think is right."

Elise stared at her, her pretty features falling as if she was going to shed those tears. "I hope he knows what a gem he has in you."

She hoped so, too, because she was putting that relationship on the line to do what was right.

Chapter Thirteen
MJ

MJ finished the last of the clean-up, taking her steaming mug of peppermint tea to the kitchen table where a notebook and pen waited for her. Outside, the first softness of evening had started to fall in the mountains on this, the penultimate day of the year.

Since Cindy was out with Jack for a trip into town, she had time to concentrate on party plans.

Settling in her chair at the table, she looked down at her to-do list. The gathering would be intimate, mostly family, but no one had a clue that the event was anything other than a New Year's Eve party.

That meant it would be a complete surprise to everyone when Jack got down on one knee and asked Cindy to be his wife...again.

A shiver danced over her.

Was there anything better in the whole world than a proposal? No. It was such a pivotal and thrilling moment, so packed with promise and hope and no one—absolutely no one—deserved that happy ending more than hard-working, good-hearted Cindy.

Well, she wouldn't mind Gracie and Nicole getting that moment, too. And maybe...

"Stop," she muttered to her imagination, which was certainly in overdrive today. She flipped to a clean page in the notebook to start a list of snacks and desserts she'd want on hand, noting what she'd have to cook.

Her pen was still while her mind...wasn't.

Was she worried about the lodge? Yes. But this felt more...personal.

She let out a sigh, tapping her pen against the notepad. Sixty-two wasn't old, but sometimes it felt like her heart had been retired, too. She'd had her one great love—George—and losing him had left a void she never expected to fill. She'd never thought she needed to fill it.

Was she worried that watching Jack slip that ring on Cindy's finger tomorrow night might make MJ ache for something—

The creak of the mudroom door and a soft shuffle of footsteps made MJ glance up, heart giving a leap when she saw Matt Walker stepping in. His chestnut brown hair was slightly mussed, and he looked more serious than usual as he slipped out of a jacket and kicked off his shoes.

"Hello." She put her cup down and straightened, smiling at him. "Is everything okay in Cabin Five this afternoon?"

Matt gave her a smile that always seemed just a touch mysterious. "I don't know," he said. "I've been in town all day. I was actually looking for you."

The words sent a little delight through her chest, though she told herself not to read too much into it.

"Well, here I am," she said lightly, forcing herself into

her usual hostess mode as she pushed up. "Do you need more towels or another log for your fire?"

He shook his head. "No, nothing like that. Well... maybe a cup of tea. And"—he slid his gaze to the frosted cookies on the counter—"one of those bad boys."

MJ laughed, grateful for the simple request. "Help yourself and have a seat. You like the lemon ginger tea, right?"

"You do know your guests' preferences, MJ. Will that go under my picture in your book?"

"I haven't taken your picture yet," she remembered, snapping her fingers. "But don't think you can get out of it. A Polaroid for every guest who's ever stayed here. Under yours it will say...lemon ginger tea, can fix roofs, and is very..."

He lifted his brows, waiting.

"Charming," she finished, smiling as she filled the kettle.

Charming? *Oh, MJ. Are you flirting?*

Maybe.

"I heard there was a lot of excitement in the paddock today," he said. "A girl in a wheelchair rode Copper?"

"Oh, yes." While she prepared his tea, she told him about Elise, loving that he listened so attentively and asked questions that demonstrated sympathy and heart.

She served him the tea and sat across from him, pushing the empty notebook to the side. The party could wait. Matt was too...important.

She wasn't sure how that had happened, but it had.

His smile faltered as he lifted the mug and looked

down at it, the softest sigh escaping. And all that did was make her want to know...why?

She normally didn't really care that much about her guests' every sigh. Oh, she worried if their rooms were warm, their bellies were full, or their beds clean and comfortable.

But she felt differently about this man, whether she wanted to admit it or not.

"Oh, I meant to tell you we've called the roofer," she said after the silence lasted a beat too long.

"And? Was I right about the support beam?"

"He couldn't come this week, but we're on his schedule for the morning of January second. I just hope it's..."

"A reasonable fix?" he guessed when she didn't finish.

"We're going to need a new roof," she said, shaking her head. "But I don't really want to think about that today."

He nodded, taking a sip. "The new year will solve all your problems," he said.

She gave a soft snort. "If only it were that easy, Matt."

He just gave a tight, impossible-to-read smile.

"Speaking of the new year," she said brightly, "we're having a little gathering, just family and friends for New Year's Eve. Will you join us?"

He raised a brow. "I'm on that VIP list?"

"Of course," she assured him. "Just a fun celebration and..." She bit her lip. "Maybe a surprise."

He leaned closer, intrigued. "You're going to have to tell me."

MJ pressed her lips together. She couldn't ruin Jack's big moment, no matter how tempted she was to share the secret. "I can't. But trust me—you don't want to miss it."

His smile faded, and he set his mug down with a quiet clink. "I mean, you're going to have to tell me because I won't be here."

Her heart thudded. "Oh. Did you make New Year's Eve plans?"

"I'm, uh..." He shifted in his seat. "I'm leaving in the morning, MJ."

The words landed like a blow. MJ blinked, trying to process them. "You are? But... Oh. That's so sudden."

"I've been here since Thanksgiving." He gave a small shrug, though his eyes were shadowed. "It's time."

She swallowed, her throat tight. "So you're going back to Florida?"

For a fleeting second, something flickered across his face—pain, maybe. Regret. Then he shook his head. "For a while, yes."

The disappointment hit harder than MJ expected. She had pictured him at the party tomorrow night, a quiet anchor amid the joyful celebration.

She'd imagined—just maybe—that the new year might bring something new for *her*, too. She was going to dress up, sip some champagne, and...have a midnight kiss?

Now *that* was taking her famous optimism too far.

"Did you know this all along or did you just decide to leave?" she asked because, honestly, she was a little sad he hadn't told her sooner.

"I just...yeah, it's time to go."

"Did something happen?" she pressed, so unsatisfied with that answer. With all his vague responses, to be honest.

He muttered something that sounded like, "Not really," and picked up his mug again.

"Matt," she said, keeping her voice level. "I don't mean to overstep my bounds, but can I ask you something?"

He looked over the rim and adjusted his glasses, barely nodding.

She chose her words carefully and said them slowly. "Haven't we become good enough friends that you can be honest with me?"

"I've never lied to you," he said simply, the statement carrying a little more weight than she actually expected.

"Well, you're not being completely honest right now."

He gave a low laugh, as though trying to defuse the tension. "Well, you're keeping secrets too, remember? You just refused to tell me what tomorrow night's surprise is." He leaned back, his tone playful but not entirely light. "People have all sorts of reasons for keeping things to themselves."

She conceded the point with a tip of her head, though her frustration simmered. It wasn't the same. Not at all. And to prove that, she took a breath, then whispered, "Jack is proposing to Cindy at midnight."

"Oh!" His eyes widened, then lit with genuine delight. "Really? That's wonderful news."

"It is." MJ's throat tightened again. "I've been...over-joyed, honestly. Relieved. I've always hoped those two would find their way back to each other."

"Engaged," Matt said, treating the word with appropriate respect. "How does that make you feel?"

"Me?" She drew back at the question. "I just told you. I'm thrilled for them. For all of us. I love having Jack back at Snowberry Lodge."

"Anything else?" he asked, his tone gentle but probing.

MJ blinked. "Like...what?"

"I don't know, maybe...that you could have something like that."

"Romance? A proposal?" She managed to scoff lightly. "I'm sixty-two, Matt. Be serious."

"I am serious." He searched her face, his gaze intent like he really wanted to know the answer to this. "Is that something you'd ever want for yourself?"

What was he saying? She tried to not give away any of the fifty emotions that were ricocheting through her body and maintain a perfectly composed expression. She tried to act as though they were talking about the weather or the cookies, not...a *romance*.

"I've never really considered it," she managed, hoping that was a neutral and natural response.

Because nothing in her felt neutral or natural right this minute.

He just looked at her. "Never? Not once? Not... lately?"

"What are you asking me, Matt?"

"I think you know, MJ."

Well, he'd be wrong about that. She *didn't* know and she hated anything cryptic, ambiguous, or confusing. "You'll need to be blunt," she said.

He didn't answer, but visibly swallowed. Maybe he was really shy. Maybe he didn't know how to say what he wasn't saying.

"Listen, Matt," she started slowly. "This friendship has meant...something to me. More than I expected. But the truth is, I hardly know anything about you, and you know my whole life story. You've listened a lot, but haven't told me much. Nothing deep, anyway. And now you're leaving."

"Oh, there's nothing to tell."

"No, that's not true." She leaned forward, a bolt of determination shooting through her. "Start with who are you."

"Who I—"

"What is your story?" she interjected before he could derail her. "Why did you stay here all these weeks, alone? And, excuse me for my inexcusable directness, but where did you get all this money if you were just a plumber?"

Her words tumbled out in a rush, years of carefully measured composure cracking under the weight of his vague and cagey responses.

He didn't say a word in response.

"Do you have any idea how frustrating this is?" she asked. "To care about someone who *has* to be hiding something?"

His expression fell and he reached over the table and put his fingers over hers.

"MJ," he said, his voice as gentle as his touch. "I'm so sorry. But some things can't be explained. Not yet."

Her gaze dropped to his hand, seeing his wrist, where the gleam of his watch caught the light.

"How about the fact that the back of your Rolex says Graham Walker? Can you explain that?"

"It's my"—he tugged his sleeve over the watch face—"legal name."

"Okay. Why do you go by Matt? Is that a story about your past you might share? And why did you pick this lodge? Can you tell me that? And—"

He put a light finger over her lips, the touch nearly sending electricity through her, and instantly stopped her words.

"Would you give me one year?"

"Excuse me?"

"Just one year," he repeated. "Would you...wait for me?"

"Wait for...what? Why?"

He closed his eyes, clearly struggling to find the right words. "You're right, MJ. I'm not being completely honest, but I promise you, I have a good reason." He sighed, then took her hand again. "I need one year. It'll take that long to..." He swallowed. "I need to...change my life."

"Change your life? How?"

"I have some...things." He exhaled, in obvious torment. "Things I need to...to...get rid of—for lack of a better word—before I can be the man I want to be...for you."

Chills rose over her arms. Was he married? Was a wife something he needed to get rid of? Was a divorce what would change his life? That would take a year. Or maybe he had to do time for something he'd done?

Was Matt a *criminal*? About to go to prison? Or... maybe it *was* witness protection.

"What are you talking about, Matt? You have to tell me."

"I can't," he said. "You'd never look at me the same and I need you to...like me."

"I do like you," she replied. "At least, I did."

"Then you can again. In a year."

"Matt—"

"I like you, too, MJ." His thumb brushed her knuckles, his eyes fierce and earnest. "But I have a...a burden I have to deal with before I can start something real. Please. Just give me a year."

"I don't know if I can do that without answers."

"You'll get the answers," he said, anguish threading his voice. "Until then, can you trust me?"

Honestly, she wasn't sure, but she was certain of one thing—her heart was tearing in two.

Their gazes locked, and for a heartbeat, it felt like the whole world held still. Then, slowly, he leaned in and pressed a tender kiss to her forehead.

"Goodbye, Mary Jane."

She couldn't speak. She sat frozen in shock and sadness as he stood, hesitated, then walked back to the mudroom, donned his jacket and boots, and stepped outside.

When the door clicked shut, MJ sank back, staring at the empty room and closed door, feeling a hollow, heavy ache in her chest.

Tears pricked her eyes, and she pressed a trembling hand to her mouth. Tomorrow night, the lodge would be filled with laughter and celebration. Jack and Cindy would start their new life together.

She needed to cling to that, not her girlish hopes of...a midnight kiss.

MJ closed her eyes, letting a single tear slip free.

Chapter Fourteen
Nicole

Nicole wrapped her hands around the warm paper coffee cup, blowing across the dark surface before taking a careful sip. Steam curled into the cold morning air as she stood near a low stone wall, surveying the small campus spread out before her.

Great Basin Veterinary Institute in Eagle Mountain wasn't flashy or sprawling, barely the size of a community college. It had a comfy, purposeful feel—just five brick-and-stone buildings arranged around a tidy courtyard, with walking paths dusted by the recent snow.

Beyond that, a small animal hospital gleamed with glass windows, a sign over the entrance announcing it was open to the public for everything from vaccinations to emergency care. A few hundred feet away stood a long, low barn with a covered paddock, the sound of a horse whinnying carrying faintly across the crisp winter air.

At the edge of the campus, there was a tiny coffee shop with a green awning that seemed quiet on this New Year's Eve morning, but Nicole could imagine it bustled with students on a class day.

There was even a fenced park area that was clearly designed for both two- and four-legged members of the student body. Calm today, but she knew that when the next semester started, GBVI would hum with purpose and passion for animals.

Just like Elise Hale would if she were a student here.

Assuming she was accepted, assuming she was safe, assuming it was affordable—and Elise seemed certain of all those things—why wouldn't the family want her to start her life here? Surely, they couldn't want that bright and beautiful creature trapped in Heber forever?

While it wasn't really Nicole's business, she couldn't help wondering. She had a vested interest.

She closed her eyes for a moment, breathing in the clean scent of snow and pine, and imagined Elise wheeling along those pathways, bright-eyed and independent, surrounded by others who shared her dream. It felt right. It felt *possible*.

She paced slowly, sipping her coffee. That morning had been a whirlwind—she'd driven to Elise's house and arrived just after eight, missing Cameron by minutes, she learned.

That left an unsettled feeling, but she tamped it down, concentrating on figuring out how to drive the family's specially modified van. Elise knew everything, of course, and proved over and over that she was a competent and bright young woman with one problem—her legs were paralyzed.

"I'm not dead," she'd repeated to Nicole. "Just the nerves in my legs are. I'm so sick of being babied!"

Nicole understood and sympathized, which was the only reason she'd risked her budding romance by going directly against Cameron's wishes. He'd never been a twenty-four-year-old girl, and Nicole had.

Still, once they were home, Nicole wanted Elise to tell him everything, whether or not she got into the program. If the timing worked out, Nicole would tell him herself, but she couldn't hang around long, since she wanted to make Benny's dog thing this afternoon.

Bubbling with the stress of it all, she paced the sidewalk, too wound up to sit on a bench.

After what felt like an eternity, the frosted glass doors of the administration building swung open, and Nicole's breath caught.

Elise rolled out, her face luminous with joy, her pale locks tumbling over her shoulders as if even her curls were celebrating. An older man walked beside her, silver-haired and serious, his hands clasped behind his back.

"Nicole!" Elise called, her voice breaking with exhilaration.

Nicole hustled forward, trying to read Elise's expression. "How did it go?"

"Slayed it!" Elise turned to the man. "Didn't I?"

"Absolutely," he agreed, extending his hand to Nicole. "Dean Luis Mendes."

"Hello, I'm Nicole Kessler." Nicole shook his hand, impressed by his kind, steady gaze. "Thank you for seeing Elise. I know it's New Year's Eve, and—"

"Thank you for bringing her," he countered, smiling at Elise. "Don't make us wait long to sign that acceptance letter, young lady. Classes start January fifteenth."

Nicole's jaw dropped. "Wait—you got in?"

Elise's cheeks flushed pink, her eyes shining. "You are looking at a new student on the spring semester roster of GBVI! Can you believe it?"

Nicole dropped to her knees beside the wheelchair, hugging her fiercely. "Of course I can believe it. You deserve this so much."

Dean Mendes gestured toward a three-story brick building across the courtyard. "Why don't you two go take a look at the housing? You'll want to see where you'll be living. Here's a master key card to enter the handicap-accessible apartment." He slipped a card into Elise's hand. "First floor, end of the hall. Everything's been customized for full independence. Go check it out and start planning your décor. And pets are more than welcome, of course. You'll find plenty of service animals at Great Basin."

"Thank you," Elise whispered, clutching the card as though it were solid gold, then she looked up with narrow eyes. "You, dear sir, are truly open-minded. I am so grateful that you see me as any other student who walked into your office."

"You aren't like any other student, Elise," he said. "And that's exactly why we want you here so much. Like I said, I would very much like to meet with your family, too. I know you are an adult, but I want to assure them you'll be in good hands and getting a great education."

"I'll talk to them," she promised as they shook hands.

Nicole's heart lifted with hope, and at how good it must feel for Elise to know she could have a meaningful, productive, and exciting future.

After they said goodbye, the two of them headed to Aspen Hall, which really looked like any suburban apartment complex, not a dormitory.

Inside, it was bright and modern, with sunlight streaming through wide windows into a cheerful lobby. The walls were decorated with student art—paintings and photos of beloved animals.

"This place is well-funded," Elise said as she rolled past a giant silk Ficus tree and headed for the hall. "Dean Mendes was telling me that fundraising is huge, and tons of local ranchers support the program, and the Department of Agriculture matches most donations. The cost will be essentially covered by scholarships and grants."

"Getting in here is a coup," Nicole said, and meant it.

As they headed down the hall, Elise's hands wobbled on the wheels of her chair, her excitement so palpable it was contagious.

"I can't believe this is real," she murmured, breathless.

"It's so perfect for you," Nicole said. "Right here on campus, surrounded by everything you need."

When they reached the designated apartment, Elise swiped the key card. The door whooshed open—a beautiful feature—and she rolled inside, and Nicole followed.

The sweet little unit took their breath away. It wasn't fancy, but it was exactly what Elise needed: an open-concept layout with wide doorways, low counters, and plenty of space to maneuver her chair. The living area had a sliding glass door that led to a tiny enclosed patio, sunlight glinting off the snow outside. A compact kitchenette lined one wall, with accessible drawers and appliances—microwave and oven at just the right height, a side-opening oven door, even a lowered sink.

The bedroom held a low platform bed with sturdy grab bars nearby. The bathroom was the real marvel: a roll-in shower with no lip at the base, a secure fold-down bench, and adjustable showerhead. Grab bars were installed strategically around the toilet and sink, every detail designed for independence.

"It's...it's perfect," Elise whispered, tears pooling in her eyes. "I can do this, Nicole. I can live here on my own. And never in my entire life have I wanted anything so badly. The last time I did? It was to get up from a hospital bed and walk."

Nicole's throat tightened as she reached down to hug Elise. "Honey, you deserve this."

"I'll work so hard and do so well in school," she whispered, almost as if she was practicing a speech she'd have to give later. "I'll be the best vet in the world."

"I know you will."

On a happy sigh, Elise wheeled herself into the bedroom, running her fingers along the dresser's edge. "I'm going to hang sheer curtains right there," she said, pointing to the window. "And maybe a photo wall above the desk. Oh, and look at all this natural light! It feels so open and welcoming."

Nicole took a few photos on her phone, already imagining how she'd show them to Cameron later as proof of how safe and supportive this environment was. Surely he'd see that this wasn't dangerous or reckless—it was Elise's chance to thrive.

Reluctantly, Elise agreed it was time to go. "I want to tell him right away," she said, rolling back toward the door. "If I can get Cameron on board, I know my parents will follow. Cameron's the key to getting them to see the light."

"And he will," Nicole said with determination. "When he sees all of this? How could he not?"

After they'd finished, they returned to the van in the admin building lot. Nicole helped Elise position her chair on the hydraulic lift platform. With a smooth hum, the lift raised her to the vehicle's interior. Elise rolled into the designated space, locking her wheels before Nicole secured the straps that held the chair steady.

Already comfortable with the van, Nicole climbed into the driver's seat, setting the GPS for the route back toward Heber City.

"We've got plenty of time," she said, glancing at the clock. "I'll get you home, then head straight to Benny's dog talent show. Then you and Cameron will both come to tonight's New Year's Eve party, and if you haven't persuaded him by then, I will. You *are* coming, right? You're not too tired?"

"Are you kidding? I haven't been to a New Year's Eve party in...forever." She snorted. "And I mean that literally. Will there be any cute single guys there?"

Nicole laughed. "Um...Red?"

"Oh, Red. Kindred spirit. Okay, I'll hang with him, but I really was hoping for someone under thirty."

"Well, there's Benny, who *acts* thirty. But he's ten."

Elise grinned, then looked out the window as they drove away from the small campus. "Oh, Nicole. I am so happy, I can't even put it into words. This is really happening. My whole future—"

A sudden, loud *thunk-thunk-thunk* cut her off, followed by a sickening grinding sound. The van lurched to the right.

"Whoa!" Nicole fought the steering wheel, heart hammering. She eased the vehicle to the shoulder, found the hazard lights, and cut the engine.

"What happened?" Elise cried, gripping the armrests of her chair.

"Not sure, but we might have a flat. Hang on."

Nicole jumped out, boots crunching on snowy gravel. Cold wind slapped her face as she rounded the back of the van—and her stomach dropped. The rear tire on the passenger side sagged completely flat, rubber shredded and steaming slightly from friction.

"Oh, dang it!" She bent closer, as if staring could magically fix it. "It's totally blown."

She went back and gestured for Elise to lower the window.

"Flat as a pancake," she told her.

"Can you...fix it?"

Nicole let out a helpless laugh. "I can barely change a light bulb, much less a van tire. And this thing probably needs special equipment. And I don't have my AAA card, which is in my car...at your house."

"What do we do?"

Nicole pressed her hands to her temples. She could call her dad, but...no.

There was really only one option. She climbed back inside, meeting Elise's wide, anxious eyes. "We call Cameron. Maybe he can sneak out of work or get me his AAA card number or a tow or something."

Elise paled. "Nicole, no—he'll—"

"He'll help us," Nicole insisted as she tapped his name on her phone and pressed it to her ear.

He answered on the second ring, his voice clipped. "Nicole?"

"Cameron, thank God. We've got a flat tire—"

"We? Who? Where are you?"

"With Elise in the van, in Eagle Mountain."

The silence lasted so long she thought the call dropped.

"You took her to Eagle Mountain?" he ground out the question. "To that vet school? Are you kidding me? You took her all the way there?"

"Look, it's a long story and we'll explain—"

"You don't have to, I already know her story." She could practically hear him steadying his breath to tamp down his anger. "Send me a pin of your location. And then do not, for the love of God, move that van."

Nicole swallowed hard. "Yes, but—"

And then the call ended...on purpose.

Nicole stared at her phone, pulse pounding. "Well," Nicole said softly, her throat tight. "That went...badly."

Elise sighed. "I've tried and begged and failed to make

him see my side. I wanted to get him out here to see the place but he wouldn't come. I tried to get him to bring me to an interview, but..." She groaned. "Now he's mad at me."

"Oh, he's mad at me, too," Nicole said.

And she understood that. Maybe she'd gone too far, violated his trust, and taken sides in a family dispute where she had no right to be.

Then she looked up in the rearview mirror at Elise—beautiful, sparkling, clever Elise who had a dream and a chance to make it come true.

She'd fallen for Cameron, but she'd fallen for his sweet sister, too.

Closing her eyes, she dropped her head back as cold dread seeped into her heart. "I just hope," she whispered, "our relationship can survive this."

NICOLE KEPT the inside of the van warm with the engine running, but the euphoria had dropped considerably as they waited. Nicole sat in the driver's seat, her hands gripping the steering wheel. Elise was silent behind her in the large middle space specially designed to accommodate a wheel chair, glumly looking outside at skies that threatened snow.

They'd talked for forty minutes, mostly about Cameron's abject refusal to consider this opportunity, but even the loquacious Elise was out of words.

Nicole's thoughts spun like the first flurries that blew past the windshield.

This morning had been filled with hope and promise, Elise glowing with excitement as they'd toured the campus. Now, that all melted away into icy dread.

She glanced at the clock on the dashboard. Cameron should be here any second. Her stomach twisted at the thought of seeing his face, of witnessing that anger she'd heard through the phone.

A minute later, Nicole's breath caught at the sight of his slate gray Tundra pulling up behind them, crunching on the shoulder. Her pulse hammered as he cut the engine, flung open the door, and climbed out. He was still in his red and black ski patrol jacket, snow-dusted boots slamming against the frozen ground. His face...

Her heart plummeted. His face was a storm.

Before she could open the door, Cameron yanked the back door, whipping it open to come face to face with Elise.

"Seriously?" he spat the words. "Why would you do this?"

"Because I want—"

"I know what you want, Elise," he fired back at her, throwing his hands wide. "And I want a lot of things I can't have, either."

"Like what?" she demanded. "Like a job? Oh, you have two amazing jobs. Friends? Yes, you have a ton of them. A relationship?" She glanced at Nicole. "I guess I may have ruined that."

His eyes shuttered, silent.

"No, I did that myself," Nicole said, flipping the handle to climb out. "Can we just fix the flat? I have a dog talent show to get to."

As her boots hit the ground next to him, she looked up, meeting hurt and anger and dismay in his blue eyes.

"Let me get my tools. And here." He shoved keys in her hand. "Take the truck back to our house and get your car. I assume you left it there when you two sneaked off like a couple of teenagers going to a party."

"Teenagers...going..." Nicole stuttered, a little speechless. "Are you kidding me right now?"

"Just go and make the dog show thing," he said, working hard to keep anger from his voice and mostly succeeding. "I'll take care of Elise."

He pivoted, marched back to the truck and pulled a toolbox and a jack from the back. Nicole stayed right where she was, watching him.

His movements were crisp and decisive, his jaw set hard, his nostrils occasionally flaring as he worked and battled the cold, getting down next to the rear passenger wheel. Nicole walked behind him to watch, refusing to drive away, but he didn't talk to her.

Elise rolled down the window on the passenger side and called out, "Cameron!"

He looked up, frowning, then jogged right past Nicole to the window. "You okay?"

"Yes! That's the whole point of this," she insisted. "I'm more than okay. I'm capable. I'm strong. I'm smart."

"You're paralyzed from the waist down," he said, his voice oddly calm. "And sneaking off with someone who's not in our family driving the van. Do you realize what could have happened to you? On these mountain roads? In the snow? It's exactly like—"

"It's *nothing* like that," she fired back. "We're not in an ice storm going through treacherous canyons. We're driving clean highways out to Eagle Mountain, and I *had* to go. I had to. Cameron, I was accepted into the program!"

He took a step back as if her words had physically smacked him. "You...were?"

Nicole fisted her hands in her pockets, frozen without gloves but she still could feel her nails digging into her palms as she forced herself not to march forward and tell him everything.

This wasn't her fight—it was Elise's. But it told her a lot about Cameron. A lot about how he handled conflict and a crisis.

"Well, that's..." He huffed a breath that puffed in front of him. "That's great and impossible and...and...and now I get to be the bad guy and the killer of all your dreams for a second time, Elise. Thank you so very much."

"Then don't kill them!" she yelled out.

He shut his eyes and shook his head. "Look. It's freezing out here. Let me change the tire and you...just roll up the window." He strode back to the tire, crouching down to start spinning the jack.

Nicole stood behind him, shivering in her jacket.

"Honestly, you can go, Nicole. We're fine."

"Hardly fine, and I'm not leaving you here without a second vehicle until you fix this."

His shoulders dropped, the move nearly imperceptible, but she picked up the resignation. He was a first responder —smart enough to know she really did have to stay.

Nicole swallowed her fear and stepped closer anyway, the mountain of apology she'd had ready dissolving in the face of his anger. He hadn't given her a chance to apologize, so how or why should she?

"We need to talk," she finally said.

Cameron's jaw tightened, but he didn't argue. He pushed up and stalked to the back of the van, yanked it open, and flipped a panel to reveal a spare tire.

"Talking is not a good idea," he said.

"Why not?"

"I'll say something I'll regret."

"I don't care," she shot back. "Just say *something*. It's bad to say nothing. That's what killed my parents' marriage ten years ago."

He froze for a second, then continued his mission.

The wind cut through Nicole's coat as she stood beside him. Gray clouds swirled overhead, matching the churning turmoil in her chest.

"I feel lied to," he muttered, bent over the wheel.

Even with the wind, she caught the words. "No one lied."

He looked over his shoulder. "Omission."

She couldn't argue that. "I understand and I'm sorry, Cameron. Elise—"

"Doesn't know what's good for her."

"Or maybe *you* don't." She crouched down next to him, flinching when he slammed the jack into place.

"You are seriously overstepping," he ground out, sliding a look at her. "I know she's irresistible and sympathetic and persuasive and *adorable*."

"She's not a minor," Nicole pointed out, frustrated that he seemed to forget his sister was an adult.

"No, but she's paralyzed and vulnerable and...and...if there's a fire, she couldn't get out of bed. If there's an intruder, she couldn't defend herself. If there's a—"

"I get it." She put a hand on his arm. "I totally get that. She's limited in what she can do. But does that mean she can't *live*, Cameron? She can't leave that house? She can't study and have a profession or achieve a dream?"

He sighed. "I'm not discussing this now," he said. "The bottom line is you went way beyond...just too far. Too far. Behind my back, too."

He slammed the spare into place.

'I'm sorry," she said, and meant it. "I was uncomfortable with that, but if I hadn't, she'd have missed the interview and—"

"Uncomfortable?" His hands froze. "You know what's uncomfortable, Nicole? Knowing that because you were an idiot, your sister will never walk again. I live with that every day, so if I fear for her life, that's my problem."

"You made it her problem."

He grunted. "Just...let me work. You have no idea what I deal with every day. You have no idea how terrified I am that she'll get hurt again."

She stared at him for a long, long time. "You know which one of you is really paralyzed, Cameron?"

Slowly, he turned to her.

"You," she said. "You are paralyzed by fear and I say that as someone far too familiar with the feeling. And your fear is keeping her from having a life. Not her legs, not that chair, not this world. Your fear."

He closed his eyes and tried to swallow. "Please wait in the truck," he said. "When I'm done, you can go."

She pushed up and took a step backwards, a bone-deep disappointment kicking her in the ribs. "So...what about us? All done?"

His hands moved with furious precision as he cranked the jack and wrestled the spare tire into place. The cold wind whipped around them, carrying the metallic tang of true sadness.

She could feel their fragile new relationship shatter with each beat of silence, pieces scattering across the frozen ground like shards of ice.

"Cameron..." she whispered.

He twisted a bolt with fury. "There's no 'us.'"

Something inside her cracked wide open. She stumbled toward the truck, her vision blurred with tears.

When she slid into the driver's seat, the wheel was cold beneath her hands. She sat in the cab and watched him finish, return the flat tire to the back, and put his toolbox in with it.

Then he climbed into the front seat of the van, and drove off.

The hardest part was that she didn't get to say goodbye to Elise.

Chapter Fifteen

The parking lot of the Canine Canyon Animal Refuge glistened under a light snow. Gracie tugged her coat tighter and glanced around as she walked toward the main building next to her mother and Aunt Cindy.

The muffled sound of excited barking carried through the frosty air as they nodded to other parents. No sign of Sam, of course, and no sign of Marshall, either.

Nerves over seeing either man pinged in Gracie's chest, making her uncomfortable and tense about the whole day. The fact that her son had put his heart and soul into winning the contest and her grandfather had hauled out an antique popcorn maker to help the cause didn't give Gracie any more peace about this afternoon.

"I have a bad feeling about all this," she muttered, expressing her fears to the chilly air.

"Bad feeling? I don't know what that is," her mother quipped.

"Because your middle name should be High Hopes and Optimism, Mom."

Gracie expected a typical trilled laugh and a flick of her wrist, the usual MJ McBride response. But her mother barely smiled or seemed to be her cheery self today, giving Gracie another thing to add to her worry list.

"Have you heard from Sam?" Mom asked.

"Not a word." She forced a smile and spoke the inevitable words, "I'm pretty sure he's not coming."

Her mother reached over and gave her hand a quick squeeze. "His loss. Today is about Benny."

Gracie nodded, gulping past the lump in her throat. Not that she expected or even wanted Sam to come. But Benny's disappointment would be her disappointment, and she'd do anything to keep that kid from hurting.

"There's my girl," Cindy called out, slowing her step when they noticed Nicole hustling closer from another section of the parking lot. With a wool hat pulled low over her eyes, she lifted a hand and gave a lackluster smile.

They all knew she'd spend the morning with Elise in Eagle Mountain, so none of them expected her to have flushed cheeks and damp lashes.

"How did it go?" Cindy asked, concern in her voice echoing Gracie's thoughts.

"She got in." As they reacted, Nicole held up a hand. "Cameron is furious and I think we're done."

"Nicole!" Gracie slid closer, putting an arm around her. "Are you sure? What happened?"

She just gave Gracie a sad look. "Later. Tonight. This is about Benny." Looking around, Nicole asked, "Where's Dad?"

"He's coming with Red," Gracie said. "And bringing a surprise. Don't ask. It's a Red and Benny special."

Nicole gave a low groan and a dry laugh. "That usually means trouble."

"Tell me about it," Gracie muttered.

As they joined a few other parents and family members on the way inside, Nicole leaned closer to Gracie. "Is Cream Puff Guy here?" she whispered.

"Not yet."

"Did you bring cream puffs and your nerve?"

"No to both."

"Gracie! Why not?" Nicole demanded.

"I don't know. All week long, he either dropped off or picked up Olivia at different times or had an important call or...avoided me. I really don't think he's interested."

"Only one way to find out." Nicole elbowed her. "And it means one giant step out of your comfort zone. You can do it, Gracie."

"Don't you hate men right now?" Gracie asked, laughing.

But Nicole didn't even smile. "No, not at all," she said. "Cameron's not wrong and maybe I was, but he handled it poorly. And I had high hopes for Cream Puff Guy."

"So did I," Gracie admitted. "But first, I have to get through this event and I'm..."

"I know—tense, nervous, and certain something's going to go wrong."

"Why do you know me so well, Nic?"

"'Cause we're cousins. And what could go wrong? It's

Benny's brain, Sir Isaac Newton's laws, and Red's...what is he bringing again?"

Gracie's eyes shuttered. "Trouble."

They dropped the subject when they stepped into the rec room, where folding chairs were arranged in rows facing a platform stage draped with lights and garlands. Above a giant trophy that had to be bigger than some of the kids and dogs, a hand-painted sign that stretched across the back wall read:

Canine Canyon Welcomes You! Paws & Pals Talent Show!

Paper snowflakes and dog bones dangled from the ceiling, and tables along the sides were covered with hot cocoa, cookies, and raffle prizes donated by local businesses. Gracie had provided a basket of human and dog treats, which, she was happy to see, had a lot of raffle tickets.

The happy hum of voices mixed with barks from the training room, creating a chaotic but heart-warming soundtrack.

Just as they found seats and saved a few extras, Gracie's phone buzzed in her pocket. She knew who it was before she looked.

A single text glared up at her, so predictable she almost laughed. Almost.

Sam Sutton: *Can't make it today. Coco and I are gonna try to work things out.*

The words blurred as tears filled her eyes, but not for her. Never for her. Only for Benny.

She blinked them away, then whispered to the others, "He's not coming. Big surprise."

Nicole's mouth tightened in sympathy, MJ's in anger. Cindy muttered something sharp under her breath.

Gracie forced a wobbly smile. "I just hope Benny wins so he's not doubly disappointed."

Before MJ could respond, the door to the training room opened and the camp counselors paraded in with a pack of kids and at least twenty dogs on leashes. The room erupted in cheers and applause as the children scattered to greet their families.

Gracie spotted Benny instantly—his glasses askew, his eyes bright as he half-ran, half-dragged Sir Isaac Newton toward her. His face was pure, uncontained joy.

"Mom! Where's Red? Did he make it yet? Does he have the You Know What? I'm last, so I know it's going to be like the grand finale!"

"On his way, Benny." She leaned over, getting closer to her son. "Listen, sweetheart..." She took a deep breath. "I have to tell you something."

Benny froze, then straightened like a little soldier. "Dad's not coming, is he?"

Gracie's chest ached. "No, honey. I'm so sorry. He—"

Benny flicked his hand with a noisy, "Pffft. I figured he'd flake out. Doesn't matter." His eyes lit up. "Because Red's coming with Starling Superior Snacks and we worked it out so it's part of Newton's laws! This is gonna be *epic*! I gotta practice one more time. Come on, Sir Isaac Newton!"

Gracie watched him take off, biting her lip.

"Well," her mother said, "looks like nothing can keep a good man down, huh?"

A fresh set of tears welled, this time for a different reason. "You know, that kid is the greatest thing that ever happened to me and I honestly could learn a lot from him." She leaned into her mother. "He's just like you and I love that."

"Aww." She gave Gracie a squeeze. "Trust me, he didn't get those brains from me."

"I have no idea where those brains came from, but he got your heart, and honestly? Does anything else matter?"

"To Benny?" Nicole leaned over and chimed in. "Winning this contest."

"He will," MJ said, but then she made a face. "But, honey, did he say...Starling Superior Snacks? That thing is older than Red, held together with spit and toothpaste, and I can't believe it even works."

Gracie winced. "Well, it's too late now."

Some music swelled through the speakers and the crowd of about sixty or so settled down.

Once more, Gracie took a quick scan of the room and, this time, she caught the dark gaze of Marshall Hampton in the back row. She felt the heat rise in her cheeks, hoping the light was low enough that he wouldn't notice.

He just looked right at her, a beat too long. Was she imagining a message in his eyes?

"Is that him?" Nicole whispered under her breath as she surreptitiously stole a peek. "Oh, my gosh. It's *that* Marshall! You never said his last name."

Gracie turned back to the front. "You know him?"

"Marshall Hampton? I've heard of him, of course. One of my customers at the ski shed couldn't stop talking about him moving to Park City."

"Who is he?"

"Former NFL. I think he played for…I don't know. I don't follow football, but he was a big deal and he's retired and living here now." She wiggled her brows. "Quite a catch, Gracie, since he used to make them."

Taking a breath, Gracie looked again and, meeting his gaze, she lifted up a hand and fluttered her fingers. At first, he didn't smile and her heart dropped, but the corners of his lips lifted slightly in a cool, distant smile.

"I think I've fumbled," she joked.

"I don't know," her cousin replied. "He looks torn to me. Maybe he thinks you know he was a football star…"

"I had no idea." Gracie slid her a look. "But, to keep the sports analogies going, he's out of my league."

"Not at all, but—"

"Oh, here's Jack," Cindy said.

He came striding through a set of double side doors that led to the back parking lot. He slid a door stopper under one of them to keep it slightly ajar, then strode to the chair they'd saved for him, greeting Aunt Cindy with a kiss and a big smile to all the others.

"So sweet of you to come, Uncle Jack."

"I'd never miss Benny's big day. Plus"—he thumbed in the general direction of the doors—"Red needed more help than I imagined. Did you know that thing runs on propane?"

Gracie laughed nervously. "Benny's convinced Red's arrival will seal his win."

"Or blow the joint up," Jack said wryly.

Before they could say anything else, Miss Renee took the stage to a round of applause.

"Good afternoon, friends, family, and dog lovers!" She beamed at the crowd. "Thank you all for trusting us with your kids and furbabies this week at Canine Canyon."

As she talked, Gracie blew out a breath, barely listening to the pitch to rescue a pet as she thought about Sam and Marshall and...Red.

And everything in her grew tense.

Renee launched the show with their first contestant, a teacup Yorkie named Petunia who could bark "Happy Birthday" for a treat. Petunia was cute, but her owner, seven-year-old Annie, stole the crowd's hearts. She had a high-pitched whisper of a voice, wild blond curls, and patiently plied Petunia with way too many treats to get her to perform.

But the tiny dog did bark a plausible number of times to count as "Happy Birthday to you," and received great applause for the effort.

The next few contestants consisted of a toddler and his older brother, who guided a golden retriever through a mini-obstacle course, a preteen boy whose beagle, Toby, shook paws with the entire front row.

There were several furry friends who could sit, stay, beg, roll over, turn in circles, and one particularly sizeable

Labrador named Scooby who danced a waltz by holding his owner's shoulders with his two front paws.

As they neared the end, out came Olivia and Kat, whose name got a big laugh. But Olivia became quite serious as she gave a short speech about the women at the heart of the space program, featured in the movie *Hidden Figures.*

Nicole leaned closer. "Tell me this is your future stepdaughter."

Gracie gave a dry snort. "What part of 'not interested' do you not understand?"

"Then she's your future daughter-*in-law.*"

"She makes Benny crazy."

"What better way to start a romance?" Nicole teased.

Kat did her "orbiting" routine, circling Olivia while guided by a whistle that no one but the dog could hear.

After that, Olivia started a countdown from ten, the whole crowd joined in and, when they reached "one," Kat leaped—well, *launched*—high into the air and gave the trophy a high-five.

The crowd exploded with cheers and whistles. Gracie clapped but shared looks with her mother, aunt, and cousin.

They all knew she was tough competition and they might be bringing home a sad second-placer.

"And now for our final contestant, Benedict McBride and his Cavapoo, Sir Isaac Newton!"

Benny marched on stage to the polite applause, his chest puffed out, his beloved beast trotting proudly beside him. He gave the family a tiny nod, his whole face glowing.

"Ladies and gentlemen," he announced. "I am proud to tell you that Sir Isaac Newton"—he made a grand gesture toward the dog—"is here to demonstrate the three most famous and important concepts in physical science, the laws of motion, discovered by the original Sir Isaac Newton."

Laughter and more applause rippled through the audience.

"The first is the law of inertia! An object at rest stays at rest." He pointed to Sir Isaac Newton. "Rest!"

The dog dropped to the stage floor and pretended to sleep. Pulling a ball out of his pocket, Benny rolled it toward the dog, who stopped it with his nose. "Until acted on by an outside force!"

That got a noisy round of claps and Jack whistled loud enough to get Newt to rise to his feet and bark, only to be instantly quieted by a treat from Benny.

"Relax," Nicole said to Gracie. "Your son is a pro."

Gracie gave her a grateful smile and sat a little straighter, ready for the next trick.

"The second of Newton's laws is known as force and acceleration," Benny told them. "Force equals mass times acceleration!" He snapped his fingers and the dog started walking across the stage. Benny clapped his hands and yelled, "Turbo boost!"

Instantly Sir Isaac ran, then slid to a dramatic stop at the edge of the stage, which got another enthusiastic applause.

Clapping with everyone, Gracie glanced toward the door Jack had propped open, knowing it was almost time for Red's big appearance.

"Now, for our grand finale," Benny said with the flair of a magician. "Newton's third law, known simply by scientists as action and reaction. That means for every action"—he put the homemade whistle to his lips and his cheeks puffed out as he blew, making the dog bark five times—"there is an equal and opposite reaction!"

The double side doors swung open, letting in a rush of cold air and...Red.

Everyone hooted, clapped, and hollered as Santa strode in, pushing a chipped and rickety popcorn machine on iron wheels.

Most of the lettering had faded off, and steam puffed from a tarnished copper spout. But popcorn was moving through the machine, wafting enough melted butter through the air to make the room smell like a movie theater.

"Ho, ho, ho!" Red bellowed. "Let's make some noise and have some snacks!"

The audience roared with laughter and cheers as Red cranked the handle, kernels popping wildly inside the brass kettle. Around the stage, the dogs barked excitedly, noses twitching.

The barking increased with the scents and cheers, not to mention Red's overenthusiastic "Ho-ho-ho-ing" as he wheeled his way to the front.

"Wait, wait, we're not done!" Benny called.

The retriever tried to jump on the wagon, but his owner snagged him.

The beagle leaped toward Red, nearly knocking him down.

Everywhere there was noise and chaos while Benny's entire trick teetered on the edge of disaster.

"Come on, Ben," Gracie muttered, not realizing she'd taken Nicole's hand. "Get it together, buddy. Get this under control."

Benny held up the microphone and practically screamed into it. "The popcorn pops up, and the machine pushes *down!*" He flung his arms dramatically as Red tipped the kettle, sending a golden cascade of popcorn tumbling into a serving bowl. And on the floor. "Equal and opposite reactions!"

But Benny's science lesson was lost when Sir Isaac Newton spotted Red. Unleashed, he lunged forward, zoomie style, lurching toward Red but hitting the trophy instead. It toppled with a crash, the noise just enough to set all the dogs off, including the littlest one, who shot off the stage and darted to the door.

"Petunia! Someone get my dog!"

Standing now, Gracie gave Nicole a nudge. "Get the dog!" but Nicole had her hands over her face in horror.

"Do you smell that?" she cried. "It's gas!"

Propane.

"And smoke!" Aunt Cindy yelled, pointing at the thin, dark plume curling from the propane burner at the machine's base. The copper top rattled and whistled shrilly.

Someone yelled over the barking and Jack launched from his seat toward Red just as a smoke alarm sounded a high-pitched warning so loud it drowned out *everything*.

Bright white strobe lights flashed along the walls, more than a few people knocked over folding chairs trying to get up and out, and every dog in the building started barking, howling, and running for the open side doors.

"The dogs!" someone screamed.

"I smell gas!"

"Move that old thing out of here!"

Red! Benny! Gracie felt her mouth open to shout for her son, but there was no way she could be louder than the explosion of noise around her.

"Red! Hang on! I'm coming!" Jack was nearly to Red, who was surrounded by people and dogs and flying popcorn.

"Where's Benny?" Gracie hollered, trying to muscle through people and dogs toward the stage. The whole time the smoke alarm blared, deafening and frightening, terrifying everyone.

Finally, she saw him, standing on the edge of the stage, clinging to his dog, tears pouring down as he surveyed the bedlam unfolding around him as kids who'd jumped on the stage shouldered him out of the way, desperate to get to another door.

"Get the dogs!" Renee shouted. "And get out of the building!"

Benny didn't move.

Gracie tried to climb onto the stage, but she kept

getting bumped by people and dogs. "Benny!" she called out. "Benny, I'm right here."

"I've got him," a man exclaimed behind her.

She whipped around in time to see Marshall leap up in one easy move, followed by Olivia, who turned and offered one hand to Gracie, the other clinging to Kat's leash.

As she climbed up, Gracie saw Marshall swoop to Benny and lift him and Sir Isaac Newton, carrying them both to open space.

"Benny!" Gracie called, running to them, throwing a grateful, "Thank you!" to Marshall.

"I'm okay, Mom!" Benny's voice wobbled, tears springing to his eyes. "But the other dogs—"

On the floor, Red and Jack wrestled with the machine's crank. A giant mastiff ran by and knocked the whole thing over, adding to the utter and complete pandemonium.

"Mom, what do we do?" Benny cried, trembling. "They're all running away!"

"The whistles!" Olivia shouted, handing Kat's leash to Gracie. "Hold her. We need to go out there and use our whistles to get any missing dogs back!"

"You're right," Benny said, shoving Sir Isaac Newton into Gracie's arms. "Let's go the other way."

Without another word, the two of them sprinted off the stage to the front door, leaving Marshall and Gracie staring at each other.

"Well, I'll give him this," Marshall said. "He knows how to stop the show."

Gracie barely smiled. "I want to help them."

He scooped up Kat and nested her in his arm like, well, like a football.

"Follow me," he said, putting a hand on her back. "If there's one thing I know how to do, it's avoid a tackle."

Clinging to Newt, she ran alongside Marshall, catching sight of her family guiding Red and the wayward popcorn maker out the door. When they reached the front lobby, the smoke alarm suddenly stopped and left everything bathed in a shocking silence.

They threaded their way around families and dogs, then out to the snowy steps to spot Benny and Olivia running around with their whistles. A firetruck's siren blared in the distance as a white poodle came running. A gray pittie loped over to his owner. A little Chihuahua barked his fool head off as he scampered to the loving arms of a boy about Benny's age.

With each reunion, Gracie breathed easier until finally Olivia and Benny stopped running and blowing their silent whistles, breathlessly high-fiving each other.

"We did it," Benny said as they came back to where Gracie and Marshall waited with the dogs. "We got—"

"Can you find Petunia?" The little girl who'd launched the program whispered her request to Benny, her eyes wide and full of tears.

"Where are your parents, honey?" Gracie asked, bending down to her size.

She blinked. "In heaven," she said, and Gracie nearly swayed and fell over. "My grandma brings me here and she had to work."

"Oh." Still holding Sir Isaac Newton, Gracie put a hand over her mouth to hold back a whimper of sadness.

"We'll find Petunia," Benny said, looking around with a serious scowl. "I promise you, Annie." With that, he marched away, shoulders straight, whistle out. No, that was a *real* whistle this time. He blew it with full force.

"Attention! I need everyone's attention! Right now!"

Conversations quieted and a few families stepped out from the side doors, listening to him.

"We are missing Petunia the Yorkie!" Benny informed them with the strength and authority of a man twice his age. "Form teams. Go in every direction. No cars can move. No one leaves until we find her! Move!"

"Let's go this way, Benny!" Olivia grabbed his arm and pulled him.

"I'll stay with you, Annie," Gracie said to the little girl.

As Gracie turned, she came face to face with Marshall, who gave her a strange look she couldn't interpret.

"Can you watch Kat, too?" he said, holding the dog's leash out to her. "I'll look for the missing dog."

"Of course. Come on, Annie. Let's wait together."

"Benny will find her," Annie whispered, looking up with a sincerity in her eyes that absolutely seized Gracie's heart. "Benny can do anything. He was my favorite person at camp. He's everybody's favorite."

"He is?" Gracie felt a wash of warm pride and satisfaction. "Well, he's my favorite, that's for sure."

With her hands full of dogs and one sweet little girl, Gracie headed inside, insanely proud of her son, who might have lost the contest but certainly won at life.

IN THE TIME it took for the firetruck to come and give the all clear—with a stern warning to Red—Benny's "specially designed for small dogs" whistle brought Petunia home. Gracie and Renee were able to call her grandmother, who had to leave work to pick up Annie early.

The families and dogs were invited back into the rec room to "finish" the dog show, though most of them had left. The room wasn't nearly as crowded when they gathered, so Red took the opportunity to walk around to those who were there and personally apologize for the inconvenience.

One family that had stayed? The Hamptons.

Olivia and Marshall sat in the row behind Gracie, with Kat. Gracie introduced them to her family, and Uncle Jack instantly recognized the man who must have been a decently well-known running back for the Pittsburgh Steelers.

While the men chatted, Nicole inched over with her "I told you so" look.

"If he wasn't interested, he would have left," she murmured. "I demand you ask him for coffee."

Gracie just slid her a look, saved by Renee taking the stage again.

"Well, that was eventful," she said, not bothering with a microphone. There weren't enough people to require one, and the remaining dogs were sound asleep at their owners' feet. "The trophy may have toppled, but it didn't break. We'd like to award it to the most outstanding combination of training and tricks."

Benny looked at Gracie, the competitive spark gone from his eyes. "'Sokay, Mom," he whispered. "Olivia and Kat deserve it. They were an outstanding combination."

"So that award," Miss Renee continued, "goes to Olivia Hampton—"

Benny gave a gracious, "Woot!" and clapped, turning to smile at the girl.

"—and Benny McBride."

He froze. "Me? I caused the problems!"

"Uh, I think I did," Red mumbled.

"For outstanding rescue efforts using homemade dog whistles!" Renee continued cheerfully.

Behind him, Olivia stood and gave his shoulder a nudge. "Come on, Dr. Smartypants. Sharing is caring and all that."

Benny looked up at her, a blush that he surely inherited from his mother coloring his cheeks. "Okay." He stood. "How do we share it?"

"Joint custody, like my parents do." She flicked her hand for him to come with her.

As they did, Nicole slid a sneaky glance to Gracie and lifted a brow, not having to say a word. Joint custody? Okay, he was divorced and probably, maybe, single.

While the kids accepted the trophy and Olivia gave a

short speech about teamwork with friends, the parents clapped. Red gave them a standing ovation and Jack whistled.

The whole thing ended on a high note with some cookies, lemonade, and friendly chatter.

As the small group began to disperse, it only took one more "Do it or die!" look from Nicole for Gracie to suck in a breath, tamp down her nerves, and walk over to Marshall.

He stood with his hands in his pockets, chatting with Renee when Gracie joined them.

"You two have the most amazing kids," the woman cooed. "Both so smart and resourceful. It's been a pleasure to have them at camp. I dare say they'll be counselors soon."

"Thank you," Gracie said, smiling at her. "You know I was worried about Benny making friends."

"No need to worry about that. Oh!" She pointed her cookie across the room. "There's Annie's grandmother. I'll go get her."

When she left, they stood quietly for a beat, then Marshall sighed. "Kids as smart as ours are a blessing, although sometimes I wonder what God was thinking."

She smiled. "He was thinking that we needed them to complete our lives."

His dark eyes flashed. "Olivia certainly does that for me. Although you seem to have a large and vibrant family."

She glanced over her shoulder. "Some a little too vibrant...ahem, my grandfather."

He cracked up. "He's a hoot. And Jack Kessler is your uncle? He's a local legend who was in the Olympics and on ESPN."

"I understand you're kind of famous yourself."

"Only if you follow football, and I've been retired for a while, so no autographs, please."

She smiled and saw her opening. "But you might get a free cream puff and coffee from Sugarfall. You're welcome to one anytime."

He held her gaze, a gleam in his eye that had to be...mutual attraction. "That's nice, Gracie. Thank you."

She let out the breath she'd been holding. "But...no," she finished for him. "That's fine. I—"

He held out a hand, stopping her. "Gracie, I haven't been completely honest with you. Well, I haven't had a chance but that's my doing."

"You *have* been avoiding me," she said, grateful for the honesty.

"Not you, actually. I didn't want to avoid you." He huffed out a breath, sounding almost as nervous as she was. "Because getting to know you is inevitable."

She studied him for a moment, not following.

"For one thing," he said, "Olivia and Benny will be in the same school come January. She's starting at Alpine Elementary in his grade for the next semester."

"Oh, okay. It's a great school, but..." She felt a frown pull, not sure why that would stop them from having coffee.

"For another, you mentioned the construction across

the street from Sugarfall," he said. "The renovation of what used to be a bookstore."

She paused, trying to imagine where he was going. "Are you...the contractor?"

"Owner of the new business."

"Oh? That's awesome. What is it going to be?"

He didn't answer right away, but looked...apologetic? Why? "A shop for...treats and snacks and desserts."

"Like...a bakery?" Seriously? Across the street from Sugarfall?

"More like the anti-bakery. It's called Craving Clean. I'm specializing in whole and healthy desserts and treats, all pure, no seed oils, high protein, super clean. It's my hobby and I'm turning it into a business."

She hadn't heard too much after "anti-bakery." "So you weren't kidding when you called my cream puffs deadly."

He laughed, but she could tell the conversation made him uncomfortable. "Look, Gracie, I don't want to put you out of business or take one cream puff off the market," he assured her. "Sugarfall is awesome and packed for a reason. But I just want to offer health-conscious people an alternative. I got the space for a great price and couldn't resist. I knew the fact that it was across the street from a bakery was just...ironic."

Not what she'd call it.

"Believe me, I know how hard it's going to be to launch a business," he said quickly. "I have mad respect for you, for your shop, and for the fact that you made a landmark destination in a town like Park City. I just want to do the same thing, only pull the thousands of tourists and locals who are looking for something delicious that meets...other criteria. You know, the health nuts."

And in a ski and outdoor sports town? They were everywhere.

"Well, that's...yeah. Good luck and welcome to the neighborhood."

"Thanks," he said. "But you understand why I think it's best if we're just friends. Because like our kids, we will compete and I'd like to do that with as much class as they've shown."

She certainly couldn't argue that. "When do you open?"

"Construction through spring and a soft opening this summer, officially doing business in the fall. By this time next year, I hope to be reaching every person in Park City looking for a sweet, but healthy, treat."

"Well, that's—"

"Don't say awesome, because we are definitely in direct competition. Friendly, but direct. So..."

"So no coffee," she said softly.

"I just wanted to be clear and honest and explain that under any other circumstances, it would have been dinner and hours of conversation."

She felt the old blush rise, and cursed it as always. "I understand." She glanced over at her family and caught Nicole's hopeful eye. "I'm sure I'll see you in town. And at school."

Oh, boy. She'd never escape this guy.

"I look forward to it," he said.

With the sweetest smile she could muster, she walked over to her mom, aunt, and cousin, who were just finishing up pictures with Benny.

"I'm ready to roll," she said after she posed with Benny and the dog in front of the "Moms 'n' Mutts' display.

"Well?" Nicole raised a brow. "What happened?"

Gracie just sighed and shook her head. "I'll tell you later, but I was right."

"He's not interested?"

"Actually, worse." She gave a humorless smile. "I just went from have a crush to...being crushed."

"What?"

"Come on, let's go do New Year's Eve at the lodge."

Nicole's eyes shuttered. "Can I pass? I don't feel—"

"No." MJ stuck her head between them, giving a hard look to Nicole. "You have to be there. Have to. It's going to be a big night."

Nicole sighed and looked at Gracie. "We'll just be sad together in the corner, okay?"

Gracie gave a dry laugh. "Sounds like fun."

And exactly what she needed tonight.

Chapter Sixteen

Nicole

Night had nearly descended when Nicole made her way to the far end of the Canine Canyon parking lot. Snowflakes swirled around lights like glitter shaken from the sky, falling heavier every minute. The cold air bit her cheeks as she hurried across the slick asphalt, her boots crunching over patches of ice.

The sounds and images of the dog talent show lingered in her ears—kids laughing, dogs barking, Benny's triumphant cheer echoing in the background. It had been quite the event and a great distraction from the hollow ache in her chest.

But now she had to go get ready for Aunt MJ's New Year's Eve party and all she wanted to do was climb in bed and cry.

How had it all come crashing down so quickly?

Just a few hours ago, she'd been falling for Cameron Hale—hard and fast—while bonding with Elise, his amazing, vibrant sister. But then came the fight, his words sharp and cutting, leaving her to wish she'd stayed away.

As she blinked away tears, she noticed a man standing by her car, and a dark gray truck with the lights on and exhaust coming from the back parked next to him.

Not any man. *Her* man.

She sucked in a lungful of frigid air. He looked so solid, so heartbreakingly handsome under the halo of the parking lot light, snowflakes collecting in his dark hair.

Her heart thudded painfully. *Don't hope. Don't hope,* she told herself, but it was too late.

Cameron lifted his head, his blue eyes locking on hers. He looked nervous—almost vulnerable. The sight of him like that twisted something deep inside her.

"Nicole." His voice was soft, carried by the wind. "Can we talk?"

Her feet felt glued to the icy ground, but somehow she made herself move closer. Every step was filled with uncertainty.

"I...yeah. I guess we can talk." Her tone was cautious, but her chest ached to throw her arms around him.

He gestured to his truck. "It's freezing. Come sit in my truck, it's warm."

Nicole hesitated, then nodded, climbing into the passenger seat when he held open the door.

The warmth was welcome as she inhaled the familiar scent of snow equipment and faint traces of pine.

Cameron got in the driver's side and shut the door behind him. For a heartbeat, they just sat there, staring at each other.

Finally, he reached for her hand. His was warm and strong, trembling slightly. "Nicole, I need to say this right, so please...just let me get it out."

She swallowed hard and nodded, her throat too tight for words.

"I'm sorry." His voice cracked, raw and unguarded. "I am so unbelievably sorry for how I treated you. You didn't deserve my anger. You were just trying to help Elise, and I..." He drew in a shaky breath. "I let my fear get in the way. I lashed out because I was terrified. And it was wrong."

Nicole's eyes burned, and the sincerity in his tone unraveled her completely.

"I understand why you got upset," she whispered. "I overstepped. I should have talked to you first before taking Elise to the school. I just, I wanted to help her, and—"

"No," Cameron said fiercely, squeezing her hand. "You didn't overstep. You did something incredible for her. You gave her hope. You gave her a future." His eyes shone with unshed tears. "And I nearly ruined it because I was too stuck in my own guilt to see what was actually best for my sister."

Nicole's breath hitched. "You have nothing to be guilty for."

He nodded, his jaw tight. "It's easy to say that, but hard to feel it, Nic. I was supposed to protect her. And I failed." His voice broke, raw and jagged. "Ever since then, I've been...overcompensating. Smothering her. Treating her like she's fragile, because if anything else ever happened to her, I'd never forgive myself. Never."

"Oh, Cameron." Nicole cupped his cheek, her thumb brushing away a stray tear. "Elise doesn't blame you. Not one bit. She loves you, but she doesn't want you carrying that weight forever. It's not fair to either of you."

He closed his eyes, leaning into her touch. "I know that now. Elise...she told me herself. She said I needed to stop punishing myself and start believing in both of us."

Nicole's heart swelled. What a gem that girl was.

Cameron took a deep breath, his gaze locking on hers. "And you. Nicole, you've shown me what love really looks like. You didn't just accept Elise, you embraced her. You two became such immediate friends in a way I never expected. Watching that...watching *you* made me realize how wrong I was to think no woman would ever want to take on both of us."

Tears slipped down Nicole's cheeks, hot and fast. "Cameron..."

"I'm falling for you." The words tumbled out, fierce and certain. "I think I've been falling for you since the moment you walked into my life. I was too scared to admit it, but the thought of losing you made me see how much I need you. And how much Elise needs you."

"I'm falling for you, too," she whispered, her voice trembling with the truth. "I tried to tell myself it was too fast, too soon, but yeah. I fell for you just as hard. And I love Elise. You two are a package deal, and I wouldn't have it any other way."

"She said the same thing," he admitted on a laugh. "Man, did I get an earful on the way home from Eagle Mountain."

"The school and the program are—"

"Wonderful," he finished. "I am being a selfish jerk to try to stand in the way of her doing exactly what she was put on Earth to do. But more than that, she said...what an incredible woman you are."

Nicole smiled. "We definitely bonded."

"It's more than that. She made me see what I already knew." He took a deep breath and let it out slowly. "I want you in my life in...in every way for as long as you'll stick around. I'm crazy about you and I believe I will be a better man because of you."

"Oh." She leaned into him, speechless as he pulled her into his arms.

Their lips met in a kiss that melted the world away, leaving only the warmth of his mouth and the steady thrum of wildly pumping pulses.

When they finally broke apart, breathless, he rested his forehead against hers. "I want to do this right. For both of you. I'm going to help Elise get ready for vet school. I'll talk to Mom and Dad, convince them it's the right move. And when she leaves in a few weeks, I'll be the one cheering the loudest."

Nicole's joy bubbled over. "Oh, Cameron, that's amazing! She's going to be so happy!"

He smiled, a little sheepishly. "I haven't told her yet. I wanted to do it with you there. We'll tell her together."

Her heart soared. This wasn't just forgiveness. It was a future, solid and shining before them.

They kissed again, slower this time, savoring the sweetness.

Cameron brushed a strand of hair from her face. "So...are Elise and I still invited to the New Year's Eve party at the lodge tonight?"

Nicole laughed, swatting his chest. "Of course you are!"

He grinned. "Good. Because I'm pretty sure Elise has been doing her makeup since I left, certain that I could grovel my way out of this."

"You don't have to grovel," she said. "You've been honest and...and fearless. That's what I find the most attractive about you."

"Didn't feel fearless driving here." He kissed her forehead. "But I do now."

Nicole raised an eyebrow, amused. "Oh, yeah? And how did she know I'd forgive you?"

"Because she knows you and your heart," he said. "Let's go get her, and bring you back here to get your car. Then we'll go to the party."

"Sounds like a plan."

All her sadness lifted as they drove out to Cameron's house and she filled him in on the debacle that was Benny's show. They were still laughing about Red and the popcorn machine when they pulled into Cameron's driveway. Nicole's excitement was nearly impossible to contain.

The moment they stepped inside, she gasped. Elise sat in her wheelchair near the window, dressed in a sparkly silver dress that caught the light like a disco ball. Her blond hair was styled in soft curls, and her makeup was on point, including a set of false eyelashes that were the embodiment of glamour.

"Girl!" Nicole clapped. "You look incredible."

Elise beamed, eyes bright with as much pleasure as

sparkly shadow. "Thanks! I can't remember the last time I got dressed up for a party." She glanced between Nicole and Cameron, her eyes narrowing playfully. "And judging by the way you two are standing so close together, I'm guessing you worked things out?"

Nicole laughed, her heart full. "We did. We're good. We're...together."

Elise squealed, clapping her hands. "Yes! I knew it!"

Cameron chuckled, kneeling beside his sister. "There's more. Something important. And I wanted Nicole here when I told you."

Elise's eyes widened, her breath catching. "What is it?"

Cameron took her hands in his. "It's a go, E."

"It's...vet school?" She barely breathed the words, hope flashing in her eyes.

"Yes. I'm going to help you do this. I'll talk to Mom and Dad—especially Dad—and make sure they understand this is what you need. We both know that if I let go, they will, too. And you're ready, and you deserve it."

For a heartbeat, Elise just stared at him. Then tears threatened, so she fanned her face. "Do not make me ruin this work of art that is my makeup!"

Laughing, Nicole reached down to hug her. "No crying! This is too happy."

Elise managed to blink back tears as she looked at her brother. "Camelot, are you one hundred percent serious right now?"

"One thousand."

With a whimper, she dabbed her eyes with her

thumb again. "I'm dead. No, no. I'm alive! For the first time in forever, I'm alive again!"

Cameron groaned and bent over to hug her. "I'm sorry you ever felt any other way," he whispered. "And logistics? We'll figure it all out. There will be some rules, of course—safety things. But you're going to make this dream happen. And I'm going to help you."

"We both are," Nicole promised.

Elise let out a shaky laugh, throwing her arms around Cameron for another hug. "Thank you! Thank you so much!"

Nicole's eyes stung as she watched them, her chest swelling with love for both of them.

When Elise finally let go, she turned to Nicole, her smile radiant. "And thank you. I know you had a lot to do with this."

Nicole squeezed her hand. "I'm just so glad I could help you reach for what you've always wanted."

Elise grinned mischievously. "Well, now I can't wait to make the toast at your wedding."

Nicole froze, her face flaming. "*Wedding?*"

Elise flicked her hand. "What do we always say, Nic? *Anything* is possible. Anything."

She was right. Absolutely anything was possible.

Not only had she found love, but she'd gained a new best friend in Elise. And tonight, Nicole knew, was the beginning of something extraordinary.

Chapter Seventeen
MJ

The party was in full swing, a sparkling, happy celebration with everyone MJ loved most in the whole world all laughing and talking in the great room and entry hall of Snowberry Lodge. Through the front windows, she could see heavy snow swirling in the darkness, the kind of storm that turned Park City into a life-sized snow globe. Outside, the world looked magical and serene.

This celebration was so different from Christmas morning when they'd last gathered as a family. This one marked the end of the holidays, the year, and, for Cindy, the single life.

It would be a new season around here, for sure. Would MJ get to spend as much time with her sister? Would they have to face their finances and consider selling the place? How would Jack play into that?

"You look too serious for a party, Mom."

MJ turned to meet Gracie's gaze, always struck by how the mix of brown and gold with that mysterious touch of green perfectly matched her memory of George McBride's eyes.

"Just pensive," MJ said.

"About?"

She rooted around for a neutral response. "All I have to do to, well, *un*do the holidays, honey. Putting it all up is so much more fun than taking it down."

"I'll help you," she said. "Sugarfall has all our New Year's Day orders ready to roll out, and this week is a lull for the bakery. I'm here for you."

MJ eyed her only child, sensing she wasn't quite right tonight. "What about you? You look serious, too."

Gracie brushed back some reddish gold hair. "I'm fine."

MJ knew better, but she also knew not to press her daughter at a party. Social situations weren't her favorite place and Gracie was not likely to open up until they were alone.

"We'll talk tomorrow," she whispered. "And I'll take your help on the tree. I think Cindy will be...on a cloud."

Gracie glanced across the room, but her attention fell on Nicole and Cameron tucked into a corner, looking completely smitten. They were laughing with Benny, who'd let Sir Isaac Newton sit in Elise's lap, all of them delighted with whatever the spunky young woman was saying.

"Love is certainly in the air tonight," Gracie noted on a sigh.

"For some," MJ replied.

Gracie looked sharply at her. "Mom, are you sad that Matt Walker checked out? You were spending a lot of time with him."

"Sad? Me? Honey, I don't know the meaning..." Her

voice faded. "Yeah," she admitted. "I'm a little sad. How ridiculous is that?"

"About as ridiculous as me kind of crushing on a guy who turns out not only to be a retired pro football player but about to open the 'anti-bakery' across the street from Sugarfall."

Gracie had filled all of them in on what Marshall Hampton was planning for Park City, but nothing more than that. MJ lifted a curious brow. "A crush? You never mentioned having a crush on him."

"You never mentioned having a crush on Matt," she replied with a sly smile.

MJ opened her mouth to deny it, then closed it, silent.

"It's okay, Mom," Gracie whispered, glancing at Cindy and Nicole. "This was their year. Maybe ours will be next year, which starts in"—she glanced at her watch—"very few minutes."

"Oh! I have to be ready!"

"For what? We'll kiss each other on the cheek." Gracie leaned closer. "Along with Red and Benny. All the singletons."

"No, no, I promised Jack..." She had cupcakes with sparklers on top and she wanted to ask Benny to figure out how to play "I Will Always Love You" on Red's phone after Jack popped the question. It had been Jack and Cindy's wedding dance song the first time around. And, it turned out, the words had been prophetic. "You'll be surprised," she finished, purposely vague.

Gracie gave a wry smile. "I don't think anyone's going to be that surprised, Mom. Look at the two of them."

She did, and sighed, not bothering to try to keep the secret. "I'm happy for her."

"You know, it's okay for you to think about love again," Gracie whispered. "I miss Dad every single day, but I know he wouldn't want you to be alone for the rest of your life."

"Hush, child. And even if I did...something like that, it wouldn't be with a man who could be a criminal or married or God knows what. Matt was hiding something and it was big enough for him to haul out when I pressed." She shook her head. "No, thank you."

"I get that," Gracie said.

Well, MJ didn't really get it. She didn't understand why Matt was so cryptic or why she felt so empty, lonelier than she had when George died.

And that confused her most of all. She'd loved George with her whole heart, and she'd been blessed to have him for so many wonderful years. That love should have been enough to last a lifetime.

So why did she keep thinking about those words...

I need one year. It'll take that long to...change my life.

How? Why? What did he need to do in that year?

"What time is it?" she asked Gracie, aching for a new topic.

"Ten minutes until midnight."

Just then, Jack stepped away from Cindy and navigated the small crowd to reach MJ, a light in his blue eyes.

"I'll let you two plan surprises that won't surprise anyone," Gracie teased, moving away when Benny called her over.

"You ready?" she asked Jack when he came up next to her.

"Nervous, but yeah, ready."

"Before, during, or after midnight?" MJ asked.

"I think right before. Two minutes. I propose, she says yes—God willing—we cheer, then do a countdown to midnight."

"Perfect!" MJ said. "While everyone is doing their New Year kissing, I'll get the sparklers on some cupcakes and cue my musical surprise."

"Don't tell me," Jack teased. "'I Will Always Love You.'"

MJ just laughed. "Oh, I hate to be so predictable."

"What you are is thoughtful and spectacular." Jack gave her an impulsive hug. "I've missed having you as my sister these past ten years."

"Then don't disappear again."

His smile faded. "Never, MJ. I give you my word I will not leave that woman ever again."

They shared another quick hug, then she gave him a nudge. "Get to it, Romeo."

In the center of the room, Jack tapped his glass with a spoon, and silence fell.

"Excuse me, everyone," he said, his deep voice carrying easily over the room. Cindy turned to him, surprise and curiosity lighting her features. Jack's hands trembled slightly as he reached for hers.

"I just wanted to take this time as the year ends," he began, his voice thick with emotion, "to say how grateful I am to be here tonight. To be *home*."

Everyone reacted with claps and "Aww" and "Yes!"

"Life doesn't always give you second chances." He lifted Cindy's fingers to his lips and pressed a kiss on her knuckles. "When it does..." He swallowed hard, eyes locked on Cindy's as he took her other hand. "You grab them with both hands."

She laughed at the play on words, letting him pull her closer.

"We have exactly five minutes until midnight—"

"Three and a half," Benny called out, making everyone chuckle.

"Three and a half until a new year begins. A year that I hope will be very different for us, Cindy." He took a step back and slowly lowered himself to one knee, producing a small box from his pocket.

For a few suspended seconds, no one spoke as Cindy gasped when the realization hit.

Behind them, Nicole put both hands to her mouth and stifled a whimper. "Oh...this is happening."

"It is," Jack confirmed, shooting a grin at his daughter before focusing on Cindy. "At least, I hope it is. Cynthia Starling Kessler, you are the love of my life...always have been and always will be."

"Jack," she whispered.

He opened the box and everyone reacted to the sparkling rock, which was certainly bigger this time around. "Sweet Cinnie, will you marry me—again?"

Cindy sobbed out a "Yes!" and the room erupted with applause and cheers. Standing, he slid the ring on her finger and they kissed, long and deep.

MJ swiped at tears, as did just about everyone in the room, including her father. Red and Nicole stepped closer to hug the couple, laughing, then Gracie and Benny joined them.

"Mom!" Gracie called, waving her over. "Starling family hug!"

Joining them, she kissed her sister, her brother-in-law-to-be and laughed when Benny pulled back and called out, "Thirty seconds to midnight!"

In the flash of silence that followed the next round of chatter, MJ froze, hearing a loud...pop.

She looked around for the champagne but she hadn't brought out a fresh bottle. But there it was again. And again.

The fourth noise was no champagne bottle, but a sharp, splintering crack, loud and ominous enough to bring the room to silence, every single expression registering confusion.

Another bang split the air, and suddenly there was a groan so loud and low it felt like the entire lodge was crying out in agony.

"What was that?" Cindy gasped, clutching Jack's arm.

Before anyone could answer, a thunderous crash shook the entire building. The floor trembled beneath their feet, glasses shattering, screams rising from most everyone.

"Everyone out!" Cameron shouted, diving into safety mode to order people to the front door. "Outside! Outside! Now! In a line!"

With Jack's assistance, they herded out, with Nicole holding tight to Elise's wheelchair to get her to the front porch.

"Move! Now!" Cameron grabbed her arm, but MJ was frozen in horror and disbelief.

"What just happened?" she croaked.

"I'll find out," he insisted, giving her a hard nudge. "Go out. Go outside."

She stumbled out into the cold, hands over her face, tears freezing on her lashes as the snow fell.

"Stay here!" Cameron yelled, then disappeared into the house.

The noise had come from the back of the lodge, MJ knew. Her kitchen. And she also had a really strong suspicion about what it was.

"The roof," Cindy whispered. "The roofer's coming the day after tomorrow."

MJ looked at her. "I think it's going to be too late."

A moment later, Cameron came back out, crestfallen. "The roof caved in. I think we should call 911 to make sure the whole place is secure but it looks contained to the mudroom, half the kitchen, and the apartment back there."

"I already called," Jack said, holding up his phone.

In the distance, she heard sirens mixed with fireworks that flashed in the sky.

No one sang "Auld Lang Syne." No one kissed. No

one cheered. No one ate a single sparkler-topped cupcake.

As the clock struck twelve, MJ had a sickening sensation that her home, her world, and her life had just completely collapsed.

Hours later, the firefighters let MJ and Cindy take a look at the aftermath once they'd determined that the lodge was secure and the roof damage, while severe, was limited to a small section of the kitchen.

Unfortunately, that "small section" included the mudroom, MJ's living quarters, and her pantry, storage cabinets, and baker's rack.

Cindy and MJ went together, with Jack. Stepping into the kitchen literally turned her stomach.

Where just hours ago there had been warmth and light and the comforting scent of baked goods, there was now chaos. A gaping hole yawned overhead with snow pouring in like a white waterfall.

"Oh, dear," MJ whispered, her knees nearly buckling.

"We have insurance," Cindy whispered. "The rest of the lodge is totally fine. People can sleep here tonight— well, not you—but we will fix this. This could have been worse. You'll get a new kitchen. And a roof."

She turned to her sister, hearing the encouraging words she should have been saying herself. Wasn't she the optimist? Wasn't her glass half full?

But nothing felt full or optimistic right then.

"Or we could sell as-is and save ourselves a lot of headache, trouble, and money." The words slipped out of MJ's lips, so foreign it felt like someone else was saying them.

"Not tonight," Cindy replied. "Let's get the photo albums in the cabinet and some clothes for you. You can sleep in Cabin Five since it's empty. I'll stay with you."

"I will, too, Mom," Gracie said. "Red took Benny up to our house, and Nicole is with Cameron and Elise, all of them staying in the ski shed tonight."

MJ looked around, noticing most of the guests had gone to rooms or cabins after they'd been cleared. She had no fight left in her. No hope. No...nothing.

Moving through the motions like a zombie, she and Cindy, with the help of Jack and Gracie, got what they could, donned jackets, and headed to Cabin Five.

"Oh," MJ groaned as she unlocked the door. "I haven't even stripped the bed and put on clean sheets."

"I'll do the sheets, Mom," Gracie said.

"Yeah, we got this, MJ." Cindy hugged her as they trudged to the cabin.

"Don't you want to be with Jack tonight?" MJ asked. "You just got engaged."

"You need me more," she said. "Sisters before misters."

That made MJ smile for the first time since the proposal.

"Relax, Mom," Gracie added, guiding her into the cozy one-bedroom. "We'll get everything ready and no one is going to leave you alone tonight. Are the sheets in the bathroom closet? I'll go change the bed."

"And I'll make a fire," Jack offered.

Sighing, MJ turned to Cindy. "Why do I seem more upset than you are? You're the numbers person."

"Because Nicole told me three simple words just one minute before Jack proposed—*anything is possible*. Right now, I believe it. Yes, I'm wildly in love and back with my favorite guy"—she smiled at Jack and lifted her newly decorated left hand—"but I know we're a family and this lodge is in our blood."

MJ didn't argue, but let them bustle about, getting the fire going while Gracie worked in the bedroom and Cindy made some tea. Jack slipped out to talk to Cameron, who was still with the firefighters, and MJ dropped into the cozy chair by the hearth.

Cindy handed her a steaming cup as Gracie stepped out of the bedroom, holding something.

"Mom."

Sipping, MJ looked up, not able to read the look on Gracie's face. "What is it?"

She held out a thin white envelope. "I found this under the pillow. It has your name on it. I think Matt left it for you."

Her heart leaped. He'd left her a letter? She sat up a little straighter and set her teacup on the table next to her, taking the envelope.

It wasn't thick, so his final words weren't too long. "I'll read it tomorrow."

"You will not!" Gracie and Cindy said in perfect unison.

"We'll leave for five minutes to give you privacy," Gracie said.

"Then we'll read every word after you do," Cindy added.

They scooted out, grabbing jackets, leaving MJ alone with what she assumed was a classic "Dear Jane" letter.

"Well, maybe I'll finally get the truth." She slid her finger over the sealed back and pulled out a single piece of paper.

Sighing, she unfolded it, angling it toward the fire for the best light on her old eyes.

Dearest Mary Jane,

She swallowed at the salutation and closed her eyes, steadying herself before she read more.

Six months ago, I walked into a gas station in Ocala, Florida, on my way home from a plumbing trade show. On a whim, I bought a lottery ticket. A few days later, I found out I was a millionaire many, many times over.

From that moment on, my life changed—and not in ways I ever wanted.

People I barely remembered started showing up, each with a hand out and a story about why they needed just a little help. My ex-wife and her daughters came knocking, too, demanding more and more and more. Overnight, the work I'd done my whole life—fixing leaks, unclogging drains, showing up for folks who counted on me—suddenly seemed...small. I didn't know where I fit anymore.

I tried to live like a rich man. Bought a Rolex. Filled my closet with fancy clothes. Splurged on sports cars, vacations, and a house that felt like a big, cavernous prison. I didn't know who to trust, where to turn, or what to do. All that money brought me nothing but emptiness.

So, I did the only thing that made sense—I ran. I went somewhere far away, a place where no one knew my name or my bank account balance. I decided to go by my middle name, left no credit card trail that anyone could find, and hid in the mountains of Utah so I could breathe again and figure out what to do with the rest of my life.

Then I met you.

It turns out the most beautiful thing at Snowberry wasn't the lodge or the view, but a woman with auburn hair and a heart so big she made everyone around her feel at home. The more time I spent with you, the harder I fell, and the more terrified I became of you finding out the truth.

I didn't want you to see me as a millionaire lottery winner. I wanted you to love me—just me. Graham Matthew Walker, the plumber.

That's why I kept my secret, even as it ate me up inside. While I was here with you, I was also quietly planning what to do with the money. I began researching people and places with the deepest needs—the kind of problems only money can fix. Hospitals, shelters, families on the brink. I've lined up accountants to make sure every penny goes exactly where it should. All those times I went to town I was meeting with a local attorney who helped me figure it all out.

I asked you for a year, because that's how long it'll take me to get it all done. A year to untangle myself from this mess, to give the money away, and to find my way back to being the man I was before that lottery ticket.

When I come back, it'll be as a simple man who fixes pipes and wants to court a classy, gorgeous, good-hearted woman the way a proper gentleman should. As far as the money, I'll keep a little bit tucked away, enough to make my golden years easier, but the rest will be gone—doing good where it's needed most.

While I do that, I want you to bring Snowberry Lodge back to its full glory and build the wedding venue of your dreams. I want you to give this historic lodge the future it —and your family—deserves.

So, please look under the sink in the bathroom, where any good plumber would leave a gift for you. The combination is 143. Maybe you can guess why I chose those numbers.

Until I come back, know this: I am and always will be...a plumber who adores you.

Matt

MJ sat stone still, holding the letter in a trembling hand. Suddenly, everything made sense...didn't it? Was this story true? What was 143? Maybe he'd left...a hundred and forty-three dollars? No, this was Matt. More like fourteen thousand and three hundred dollars.

That would come in handy.

It didn't matter—this letter gave her the answers she longed for and whatever gift he gave her, he *adored* her.

Still a little shaky, she pushed up and headed into the bathroom, pulling open the cabinet door under the sink.

Crouching down, she moved some towels and guest shampoo and her hand hit something hard.

A metal lock box.

With shaking fingers, she turned the numbers to line up to 143.

She dropped down to sit on the floor, sensing she might fall over when she opened it. Very slowly, she lifted the lid.

There, nested in a bed of green flannel, was a cashier's check made out to Snowberry Lodge for...

"Oh, my—"

MJ couldn't even touch it. Her whole body trembled as she stared at the number that did not compute in her mind. How many zeroes was that?

A million dollars?

"Hey, Mom, where are you?" Gracie's voice barely reached MJ through the noisy, slamming pulse in her head.

"MJ?" Cindy's voice rose and grew closer. "Are you— Oh." She stood in the bathroom doorway. "Are you all right?"

She turned and held up the check, a simple, life-changing piece of paper.

"Yes," she breathed.

"What is..." Cindy dropped to her knees. "MJ? What is that?"

"Proof that anything is possible," she breathed the words.

"Mom!" Gracie appeared in the doorway next, holding the letter. "He won the lottery?"

She heard Cindy squeal, falling to the floor. Gracie joined her, picking up a pack of legal-looking documents with words like "trust" and "gift tax exemptions."

"Is this even real?" Cindy asked, tears falling down her cheeks.

MJ wiped some of her own, looking at the documents, the check, and the letter. "I think all that is real." She closed her eyes and exhaled. "But the man? I guess I'll find out in a year...when or *if* he comes back."

"He'll be back," Cindy said. "He obviously loves you."

"I don't know about that," MJ whispered. "But I can't wait to find out."

🌲

MJ MAY HAVE to wait a year for her happily ever after—but you don't! Come back to Park City for another holiday filled with secrets, sisters, and second-chance romance.

After a year of renovations and redesign, Snowberry Lodge is finally ready to open its doors for the most magical Christmas season yet—and Cindy and Jack's holiday nuptials will showcase the Starling Room, a sparkling new wedding venue. The lights are twinkling, the sleigh is polished, and love is in the crisp mountain air...but not everything in Park City is picture-perfect.

Gracie's bakery is struggling, thanks to a flashy new rival across the street, and every run-in with the infuriatingly handsome Marshall Hampton stirs up more than her temper. When Benny and Olivia do some scheming, Gracie and Marshall are forced to team up—while trying to ignore the sparks flying between them.

Cindy has handed over the lodge management reins to Jack, and is launching Snowberry Weddings, a brand-new business to match her brand-new marriage. When an opportunity arises that could catapult that new venture, she learns that success might come at too high a price.

Through it all, MJ counts the days until the return of the man who made her heart soar with promises. But each snowstorm and silent night makes her wonder if it was all just a dream.

Filled with romance, laughter, and a dash of holiday magic, don't miss *Mistletoe in Park City*, the third heartwarming installment in the Christmas in the Canyons series.

Christmas in the Canyons by Hope Holloway and Cecelia Scott

Sleigh Bells in Park City
Snowfall in Park City
Mistletoe in Park City
Midnight in Park City

LOOKING for another Christmas collaboration from Hope Holloway and Cecelia Scott? Enjoy a Carolina Christmas, a charming, heartwarming holiday series that will whisk you away to a dreamy winter in the Blue Ridge mountains.

Carolina Christmas by Hope Holloway and Cecelia Scott

The Asheville Christmas Cabin
The Asheville Christmas Gift
The Asheville Christmas Wedding
The Asheville Christmas Tradition

If you're in the mood to bask in the sunshine of a gorgeous beach, fall in love with an unforgettable cast of characters, and get lost in stories you cannot put down... you've come to the right authors!

Other family saga beach reads by Hope Holloway and Cecelia Scott

Hope Holloway

Coconut Key

Shellseeker Beach

Seven Sisters

***

Cecelia Scott

Sweeney House

Young at Heart

***

Collaborations by Hope and Cecelia

Carolina Christmas

The Destin Diaries

***

Visit www.hopeholloway.com and www.ceceliascott.com for details about all of their books!

About The Authors

Hope Holloway is the author of charming, heartwarming women's fiction featuring unforgettable families and friends, and the emotional challenges they conquer. After more than twenty years in marketing, she launched a new career as an author of beach reads and feel-good fiction. A mother of two adult children, Hope and her husband of thirty years live in Florida. When not writing, she can be found walking the beach with her two rescue dogs, who beg her to include animals in every book. Visit her site at www.hopeholloway.com.

Cecelia Scott is an author of light, bright women's fiction that explores family dynamics, heartfelt romance, and the emotional challenges that women face at all ages and stages of life. Her debut series, Sweeney House, is set on the shores of Cocoa Beach, where she lived for more than twenty years. Her books capture the salt, sand, and spectacular skies of the area and reflect her firm belief that life deserves a happy ending, with enough drama and surprises to keep it interesting. Cece currently resides in north Florida with her husband and beloved kitty. Visit her site at www.ceceliascott.com